THE HIDDEN ROOM

Tom Galvin

For my Babs, keep on dreaming!

BABS – 1926

All old houses have secrets that seep into the stone, brick and mortar and settle there. A house, perhaps reflecting the various characteristics of its series of occupants, develops a character of its own. A new house is as characterless as a newborn child, all its stories and secrets waiting to unfold.

That was Babs' first impression of this house in this new development as she and Claire made their way up the brick walk to the front door. A party tonight, a party last Thursday, another earlier in the week. Claire could never lose enthusiasm for a good party; Babs had lately been realizing that she could. And this house, bright, new and shining, ragtime music and loud laughter pouring out of the beveled windows had, Babs concluded, no character. But then, she realized, she could have said that about herself.

"Tell me again," she interrupted Claire

who was about to raise the metal door knocker, "this guy is what level of gangster?"

"Businessman," Claire snapped, "and please stop acting like inviting you to this party was some kind of punishment. Earl is on his way up, whatever he does, so let's be friendly."

"Fine." Babs said, "I'm happy. Your mysterious underworld figure will have my full respect."

With a quick angry glance, Claire said, "Let's don't be talking about the underworld," as she slammed the knocker against the door.

A man in an ill-fitting tuxedo opened the door. Babs' first thought: " A butler is no good if he's not properly attired." She and Claire nodded and walked past him into the foyer where they saw an oriental rug framed by brightly buffed, dark wood floors. The rug could have been a genuine Asian import or a pawn shop purchase, like many of the objects adorning the large drawing room beyond.

Babs walked into the room slightly behind Clara and sized up the gathering. Tuxedoed men, some young, some with middle-age paunches, chatted together in twos and threes. They held brandy snifters and smoked cigars. The women mingling among the men were all young, none maternal, no wedding rings. This was not a party for wives. Babs was struck by an unpleasant recoiling in her stomach. She took a breath and whispered to Clara, "Here we go again."

"Earl," Clara called out, a bit too enthusiastically for Bab's taste. The barrel-chested Earl approached and hugged Clara, glancing over her shoulder at Babs.

"I see you brought a friend," he said

Clara held on to Earl's arm as she said, "Yes, this is my friend, Babs."

Earl had small, round eyes, unevenly spaced on either side of a large nose that looked to have been broken more than once. He looked Babs over from top to bottom. "Well, hello, Babs," he said while running his fingers through his thick, black hair doused with Vitalis.

Babs rejected eye contact, looking beyond her host. "It's nice to meet you, Earl. Nice house."

Earl waved his arm to usher them into the gathering. He motioned to a waiter, one who looked rented for the night. The waiter brought a tray of champagne. Earl looked at Babs and said, "Or would you like something stronger?"

Clara, still clutching Earl's arm, said, "Champagne's good for me," as she and Babs each took one from the tray. Babs was surprised at Earl's appearance given Clara's rave review of this allegedly charming, handsome young prize. She saw this man of medium height, a boxer's battered face, and a build like a bullet. She wondered if Clara saw him as ruggedly attractive. All Babs saw was the rugged. Clara had described suave confidence which turned out for Babs to be just another fellow who was street savvy and cocky. Her instant distaste for him seemed to sour the champagne. She glanced about at the assortment of tuxedoed men and thought of dressed up apes.

Clara was busy trying to hold Earl's attention with unstoppable chatter which he ignored with polite nods and half-smiles. He broke eye contact with Clara repeatedly and shifted his gaze to Babs. She in turn avoided the gaze which annoyed her with its condescending touch of lechery. But then she wondered what else could she expect, finding herself at yet another party, another of the free and easy young women who smile and flirt.

Babs' discomfort growing as she felt the eyes of the other men scanning her up and down, she interrupted Clara in mid-sentence. "Excuse me, Clara. Earl, could you point me to the powder room?"

He glanced to the stairway across the room but then said, "Why don't I just show you the way?"

"No, no, no," Babs protested. "I don't want to interrupt your conversation. I'm sure I can find my way."

As she moved up the staircase, Babs straddled some partiers sitting on the steps, sipping cocktails, kisses accompanied by lascivious laughter. She made her way past them amidst whistles and whispered innuendos and felt prying eyes tracing calves and thighs beneath her short skirt. She had fully embraced the daring trend toward shorter and shorter skirts and had laughed at the ones that ran ankle length. She has said things like, "Oh lord, fashions straight out of the 1910's!" How much more comfortable she would feel now passing these gawkers in an ankle-length skirt.

She made it to the hallway and walked to the end, past more couples, more kissing, more whispers, some moaning. She entered the bathroom, turned the lock, leaned back against the door, and took a long breath. She embraced the silence. The solitude was like a warm blanket thrown over her shoulders. Then she remembered that she had no real need for the bathroom. She had just wanted to escape the leering Earl, the paunchy men, the young female decorations. It all felt like one party too many. It wore her down.

She crossed to the sink and looked at herself in the mirror. If she splashed water in her face she knew she would have to apply fresh make-up. She abruptly splashed water in her face with abandon. She saw eye-liner dripping down her eyes, a freakish reflection. She took a long, critical look. "One party too many," she mumbled under her breath. "What have I been doing? I'm 26 years old, a 26 year old...," what did they call her kind? What term did they use to describe her ilk in the Saturday Evening Post article?" Flappers, that was it. "I'm a 26 year old flapper. How did that happen? Why did I laugh off other choices? Why did I make fun of friends getting married? I considered marriage as beneath me. How many of my old friends are married? Some are even college graduates. Why not? It's 1926. Why shouldn't a woman have a career? Why not me?"

Suddenly she caught herself sinking into

maudlin self-pity. "Snap out of it, Babs," she told the mirror as she rinsed away the eye-liner and pulled the compact from her purse. "Just get through the night. There's plenty of time for different choices starting tomorrow."

She patted her hair and rearranged her skirt. She straightened up to her full stature and reached inside to find her confidence. She turned and opened the door.

She could hear Earl's voice. He was coming up the stairs, stopping to banter with one of the seated make-out artists. Earl emitted a guttural laugh and said, "I think a cute little bird just flew into the bathroom and I'm on a hunting expedition."

She started to close the door and lock herself in but stopped short, knowing she couldn't hide out forever. She would have to face this brute and somehow get past his greasy clutches. She opened the door and re-entered the hallway. She looked to her left, her stomach churning, and found an escape route. A flight of stairs that led up to what looked to be an attic door. A place to hide for a while until Clara could come and retrieve Earl or until Earl cooled off. She opted for this brief exit and she tip-toed up the stairs. She could hear Earl's voice again, coming from the hallway as she opened the door and stepped into the attic. It was dark except for the shaft of light that came through the window from a street lamp. She stood by the door, silent and still, listening for his footsteps. Nothing. Was he still looking for her downstairs? Had he gotten distracted talking to his friends? Had he found another cute little bird more amenable to his advances? She waited. Nothing.

She shifted her weight as quietly as possible. The objects cluttered here and there came darkly into view: some boxes, a few dilapidated chairs, a hide-a-bed, a pile of old musical scores, all strewn about in no particular order. As she surveyed the objects, her eyes adjusting to the darkness, she could feel her knees slightly trembling. "There's no protection here," she told herself. "If he came up here I'm less safe than if I'd stayed among the other guests. She backed away from the door and moved slowly among the spaces between the stored assortment of junk. She really didn't know why she did this until it dawned on her that she was looking for some kind of protection: an object, a weapon. Maybe among the detritus of broken and discarded things was a golf club, a baseball bat. She swallowed a laugh as she asked herself, "Do I really think I have it in me to bash this fool in the head?"

It was then that she saw, in the far corner of the attic, a small glow of illumination on the floor. She inched through the darkness to see from where the light originated. As she approached that corner of the room, the light seemed to shine slightly brighter. She was baffled to find the hallway that seemed suddenly to manifest itself out of what she had been sure was a dead end to a four-walled perpendicular attic. She entered this newly visible hallway and saw a door at its far end, the light emanating from the crack at the bottom of the doorway. There was a transom above the door that seemed abruptly to make its presence known. It seemed to her that things were appearing in response to the movement of her eyes. Then the doorknob was clearly visible. She walked cautiously down the hall, curiosity overriding concerns about Earl. She felt drawn forward, not frightened, feeling an increase of warmth compared to the chill in the rest of the attic. She came to the door and was about to knock but then stopped. The need to announce herself, to whoever might be in the room, vanished. She knew she was welcome. She put her hand on the doorknob and turned it slightly. The door opened onto a room. She walked in.

The room, dimly lit at first, seemed to brighten as she looked around. The light came from kerosene lamps, two small ones on end tables separated by a love seat. They were seen to be electric lamps upon closer inspection. To her right and left facing the love seat were matching wingback chairs. Each corner of the near wall was lit by elegant floor lamps. Above the love seat was a painting of a seascape under a deep blue sky with pillow-like white clouds. It drew her in as she moved closer to the love seat, but her reverie was interrupted by the sound of voices on the other side of the door. Two men were talking.

"Where is she?"

"I don't know, Earl. I'm pretty sure I saw a girl walk out of the bathroom and up the stairs."

"She couldn't have just vanished."

"I could've been wrong but I was certain..."

"If you were certain, where is she?"

"I don't Know, Earl."

"Okay, I guess you made a mistake. Let's go down and ask that other one, Clara, if she's seen her."

Babs waited. She heard their footsteps as they left the attic, closing the door behind them. She was mildly frightened at first. "What's going on," she asked herself, "that they didn't see the room as easily as I had?" But the moment of fear became relief and then comfort that they hadn't found her. She felt warm and welcome in this room. It seemed to embrace her as if the room had been waiting for her. Then she saw the bookshelf on the wall to her right. She walked over. It reminded her of the wooden bookshelf in her bedroom when she was a teenager, with her poetry books, her Dickens and Balzak, and that young writer, Hemingway. How she had loved to read back in those days, before she had become bored, defiant, rebellious, tired of school, tired of her parents' rules, and before she set off to join the never-ending party. She picked a book at random, a book of poetry by a poet she'd never heard of. The book looked new, full of poems by Robert Frost. She sat down on the love seat and scanned the pages, her eyes focusing on a poem called "The Road Not Taken".

When she finished Frost's poem she laid the book on her lap and closed her eyes. "I should have taken the road less travelled," she whispered. She opened her eyes and looked to her right and to her left and straight ahead, drinking in the charm of this cozy room so pleasantly warm and clean and comforting. It felt to Babs that the past few years of her adult life found her moving from one dark place to the next. She had been living a nighttime life allowing for no daylight, no sunshine, no blue sky. She felt the book in her hand and thought about the fullness of its content. She had sought that fullness and depth and abundance when she was younger. She yearned for it now. Why not her? What prevented her from moving out of this dark world and into the daylight? She had saved some money. She was not too old to pursue an education, to find interesting work, to be useful and connected.

As the spirit moved in her it brought with it confidence, assurance. Fear fell away. Something about this room she had found, a room apparently hidden from others, had changed her. She could stay here forever but then, no, she could not. This was not her stopping point. It was her point of transition. This brightness, warmth, and comfort were not hers to keep. They were an invitation to find her own brightness on the road ahead, the road less travelled.

She stood up slowly and replaced the book on its shelf. She rose to her full stature and walked back into the attic. This time there was no hidden hallway, no light shining through the door. The attic was contained within four walls. She didn't stop to look back. She crossed the attic and opened the door that led to the stairway. She walked down to find the partiers in this upstairs area slightly more slurry, considerably less lucid, as she made her way past them to the main floor.

At the bottom of the stairs she spotted Clara. "Where have you been? Earl said you seemed to vanish. He said you'd been gone long enough that he was worried. He said he went to find you but you had disappeared."

Babs smiled, "Is that what he said? Well, it doesn't matter." She walked into the foyer and removed her coat from a wall peg.

Clara asked, "Where are you off to? The party's just getting going."

"I'm just getting going too, Clara. I've been at the party long enough. You want to leave with me? The buses are still running."

"No, I'm having fun and, besides, I can't leave Earl's party in full swing. What would he think of me?"

Babs slid into her coat and looked at her friend, "He's not worth worrying about, Clara."

"What do you mean? He's charming, not to mention handsome and, look at this house. He's obviously pretty well-heeled. You don't want to get on the wrong side of men like that."

Again, Babs looked directly into Clara's eyes. She was about to tell her about Earl, about to urge her to forget about him, to come along with her and catch the bus. Then she shook her head and looked away. "Well, I'm going," she said. "Take care of yourself, Clara."

"Babs, I just don't understand you. This is a great party. "We're having fun."

Babs leaned forward and gave Clara a hug. "Have fun, Clara, have fun. I have to go."

Babs walked to the door, opened it, and started down the walkway. There was a bus stop around the corner on the boulevard. The night sky was starless and dark as she walked away from Earl's house, but the boulevard ahead was brightly lit. She hurried her pace and headed toward the light.

EARL – 1932

Artie and Murray, the organization's grand old men, had finished their highballs and their cigars and had complimented Earl on the quality of the refreshments. They were thanking him for his hospitality and preparing to leave. As they got up from the leather chairs across from Earl's mahogany desk Earl rose as well and leaned forward over the desk. "You pay me great honor by coming to my home."

The two men responded with noncommittal nods. They were not honoring him; they were checking up on him but it was customary to play along with the polite pretense. Earl also knew what this visit was about and he had put forth his best effort to impress them. They had provided him no assurance nor had they been critical. Earl could read nothing in their poker faces as they listened to him recite numbers to justify his handling of the parts of the business that he controlled. He had assured them that liquor sales were brisk, his numbers-runners were meeting their quotas, and the dime-a-dance girls moonlighting on their backs represented a growing profit center.

Artie had occasionally responded with "hmms and "uh-huhs". Murray had made some notes on a small pad. Earl had gotten no applause from this audience, nor any boos. Now as they were leaving he felt the sweat that had been trickling down his chest.

The meeting was at an end. The butler was waiting at the front door with their overcoats and hats as they left the office and crossed the living room. Before leaving, Murray turned to Earl and said, "Make your father proud, my boy."

Earl assumed a determined expression and said, "I'll do my best, sir."

Artie added, "Your father's shoes, big ones to fill. He was one in a million."

"Yes he was," Earl agreed, bile rising in his throat.

The two old men stepped across the threshold and walked to Artie's sedan attended by his chauffeur. "He's not his father," Murray said as they drove away.

"No, but he's young," Artie said, "I'll grant you he's cocky, but maybe he'll learn."

"I know we're giving him this chance to honor his father's memory but I just don't like the kid."

Artie agreed. "I don't much like him either. His mother spoiled him. I remember seeing her brag about how smart he was and then yelling at him for some stupid thing. It must have been embarrassing for the kid."

"She went from being a mean old bag to being sweet as pie and then back to being mean again in a split second." Murray got into the car and slid across the back seat.

Artie got in as the chauffeur closed the door. "Well, Murray, like I say, we're doing it for his dad, rest his soul."

Murray said, "I know. We'll keep him on for the time being but I think we better keep an eye on this one very closely. He's not his father."

"Not by a long shot."

Earl was back at his desk drinking down three fingers of scotch to steady himself. "Those old bastards didn't say anything. Where's the praise? All I've done for this organization and they can't spare a good word?" He slugged down the last of the scotch as the phone rang.

It was Howard, Earl's bookkeeper. They had known each other since boyhood. It could be said that Howard was Earl's best friend but that would not be entirely accurate. Howard was useful. He had never been disloyal. Mostly Howard was familiar, a steady presence. Earl, however, did not really know Howard all that well. He didn't know what Howard thought, how he felt, what life was like for him because Earl never asked. Howard was good with numbers. He knew what to put in the ledger, what to keep out, what to hide. He was, well, useful.

"What's on your mind, Howard?"

"I'm calling to see how the meeting went, Earl. What did they say? Is everything good?"

Earl forced a laugh. "What wouldn't be good? The old guys know quality when they see it. They know I've got everything humming right along."

"Oh good, that's good. I was worried they might..."

"They might what, Howard?" All the tension that Earl was dousing with scotch suddenly exploded. "They might find problems? They might not be pleased? Why wouldn't they be pleased?"

"Well," Howard stammered, "no reason, just that..."

"No reason in the world, Howard. You need to stop worrying. It's aggravating when you worry about everything. The old men are happy, Howard, and keep this in mind. They are old men. The future belongs to the quick and the young. You hear what I'm saying?"

"Yeah, yeah, Earl, I do. Things are good. Of course things are good. There's nothing to worry about."

"So stop worrying. Like I tell you; it aggravates me." Earl swiveled in his desk chair and went on to another matter. How are you coming with costing out the projection room? Are we ready to get started?"

"We are. We are. It's tight. I've had to do some juggling with the finances. I'm hoping when we write some things off, we can make up some losses on the back end. It's not cheap, though, a home movie theatre."

"I'm not assuming it's cheap, but it's what I want, so choose the guys who gave us the best bid and let's get moving."

Earl didn't bother with a good bye as he hung up the phone. He stood up slowly, still thinking about his meeting with Artie and Murray. It was eating at him that not all was right. He was convinced that all should be right, that they had no reason not to be supportive, that no one could take his place. Still, there had been no praise, no words of assurance. Okay, there was a little skimming going on here and there, but not so much that they would notice, not the way Howard handled the books and, besides, even if he took a little off the top, he was bringing some healthy profits to the organization, so who was harmed. He continued on with this inner reassurance but not finding it very effective in helping him calm down. He picked the phone up again. He needed to talk to his mother. He stopped abruptly and rubbed the palm of his hand across his forehead. Why did he do that? It wasn't the first time. It was a crazy thing to do, to start to call someone who had been dead for five years. He reassured himself that he always stopped short, always came back down to earth, that it was just some impulse to pick up the phone. He didn't like to dwell on this or question himself but he could not deny how much he missed his mother's support, her words of praise. He needed to hear her say, "Nothing to worry about, my dear; nothing at all. Why does it matter if people question you? Who are these people anyway? None of them can judge you. They're not on your level. You're heads and shoulders above those fools who find fault with you. You know who you are. Who do they think they are?"

He could almost hear her voice as he stood at the desk, his hand still on the phone. Without thinking, he mumbled, "I miss you, Mama." As soon as he said it he recalled what the rest of her words might have been, the harsh, even frightening tone of her voice as she might have added, "Stop whining now, Earl. Be a man. Don't behave like a frightened child. Don't make me ashamed of you."

He closed his eyes and shook his head as if to erase the image of the woman he had just told himself he missed. He didn't want to think about her anymore right now. He walked away from his desk and gave his attention to his pet project. He decided to go up to what was now the attic but was soon to be transformed into the projection room.

Walking down the second floor hallway toward the bathroom, he turned right and climbed the flight of stairs leading to the attic. He recalled something: some vague memory he could almost but not quite grab hold of. Someone had climbed these stairs to the attic and disappeared. He could not quite remember the details. Maybe he'd been drinking; maybe it never happened at all. He let it go as he walked through the door into the attic. It was empty except for a few odds and ends the clean-up crew had left behind: a broom, dustpan, some cleaning supplies. It was ready for the contractors to build his projection room. He had heard and read about that man who was virtually taking over Chicago, Al Capone. Al had a projection room and could get access to reels of all the latest films. Earl wanted that for himself. He wanted to take his acquaintances from the world of business, of politics, friendly members of the police department to watch John Roland, Norma Shearer, the Barrymores, and Buster Keaton perform for them in his attic. He didn't know all the right people yet but he was certain that this enviable luxury would elevate him to a certain status and increase his social connections and his influence.

He flipped on the overhead light, a dim one which barely illuminated the room. He walked across the attic to the bay window built into the opposite wall. He felt confident, even powerful, as he looked over the developing neighborhood. Then he turned his eyes to gaze at the attic room imagining the rows of theater seats it would hold, the bar that would be installed along the back wall, the framed autographed photos of movie stars he would somehow get hold of and hang on the walls. He expanded his vision until he was able to see people, important people coming up the stairs, being served their choice of cocktails, taking their seats in preparation for the movie. He toyed with the fantasy image for several more seconds until it vanished into the dim light of the empty room. It was then that he saw another light coming from the corner of the room revealing a short hallway Earl had never before noticed. It startled him. How could this be? He had been in this attic countless times. How could he be seeing something up here for the first time?

The strangeness of this hallway suddenly appearing frightened him. This fear was quickly replaced by curiosity. Superstitions, belief in magic, returning spirits of the dead, all these things had long found acceptance in Earl's family. His grandmother had told him of apparitions. His mother attended séances. There had been no traditional religious training in his upbringing but belief in the bizarre and other-worldly had been almost taken for granted. And if magic were to occur, it was not unreasonable for Earl to think that it would occur in his world. He never doubted his own specialness. With growing confidence, he walked down the short hallway that ended at a doorway. He opened the door and walked into a room.

The room felt familiar: the thick, red velvet curtains covering the windows, the deep, green walls, the settee like the one his mother had lounged upon, and two dark overstuffed chairs reminiscent of the ones that use to swallow him up as a child listening to his mother talk to him. She would speak of great plans for his future and her high expectations that he would be a man of importance. As he slid into one of the chairs, he felt time going backwards. It wasn't like the parlor in the home of his childhood. It was the parlor. He breathed in the musty smell of the oriental throw rug and gazed at the soft glow of the chandelier. It was all so familiar, all so strange and yet so real. In just moments his body relaxed, his eyelids grew heavy. He fell asleep. He dreamed of his childhood, of being in trouble with his mother, being sent to his room. Then his mother would often come to his room, kiss and comfort him. He woke up. The illusion that this recently discovered room was his childhood bedroom vanished. It was just a room. He got up and returned to the main attic room. The hidden room vanished as he walked from it toward the attic entrance. There was no trace of light illuminating a hallway leading into a hidden room; it was all gone. On a whim he turned back and walked to where the room had been. To his amazement he once again saw the light, the hallway, the door to the room. He opened the door. There was the room. He exited again, walked across the attic, glancing over his shoulder to see that the light, the hallway, and the room had once more vanished. He turned toward the disappearing room, walked in that direction. Everything appeared again. "Astounding", he told himself out loud; "magic!" His grandmother and mother had been right to believe in spirits and visions. He began to swell with self-importance. This magic was meant for him; he had been chosen for it. He was no longer a simple member of a normal world. He had just been invited into the world of magic. But what did it mean, this room, this special

place that was meant for him? Was it a portal into time travel? Was it a place where he could work more magic? Would visions appear? Perhaps, but these possibilities were shrugged off. Magician though he may have just become, he continued to be a practical man, a pragmatist. He lived in the world of affairs and his particular calling took him into challenging, sometimes dangerous places. These were places where survival depended on many things and not just savvy and skill. Weapons were essential; stashes of off-the-books cash could purchase security; hiding places for hasty retreats might prove necessary at certain points. Was this his own personal hiding place? He would know when the carpenters came to start work on the projection room. He would find some excuse to bring Howard up here, or the butler. Would any of them see the light, the hallway, the room? He doubted it. He was the special one, the magic one. This room was meant for his eyes only.

Over the next three weeks a dark attic formerly full of storage items was transformed into Earl's personal screening room with bar, leather settees and chairs, elevated floor upon which each row of seats rose slightly higher than the row in front of it, and, of course, the cherished collection of movie poster wall hangings. Most important to Earl, no one involved in the project could see his private room.

The old men, however, Murray and Artie, did

see something. They saw the son of a powerful father who did not measure up. They saw a young upstart equipping his home with a personal movie theater as if he were Al Capone from Chicago. Impatience was growing; revenue from Earl was not.

"The kid's got a big head," Artie said, blowing on a spoonful of minestrone.

Murray picked at a salad as the two waited for the pasta. Gianno's Italian Restaurant had been their meeting place for a long time, back to the days when Earl's father was alive and the three of them were building a thriving enterprise they paid the police to ignore.

"I blame his mother," Artie said.

"Well, Artie, his mother's dead so I blame the boy. For whatever reason he got to think of himself as such a big shot, I don't need to know. What I know is that we've got young talent better qualified to run the kid's operations than this kid, and yet the dumb bastard goes ahead and builds a movie theater in his attic."

"You're right, Murray," Artie said, "No argument here. If his percentage of the take can allow such lavishness, why aren't we realizing a bigger profit at our end?"

"Good question," Murray said, "I think we need to have a little talk with Earl."

Artie shook his head. "No, we'd get better information from that bean counter who works for him, that kid, what's his name?"

"Howard," I think.

"That's right, Howard. I think we need to have a little talk with Howard. I don't think he's the type to hold back information when a little pressure's applied"

Murray smiled as the pretty young waitress brought their pasta. He told Artie in a low voice, "I'll set it up for this afternoon."

It was early evening when Earl's butler opened the front door and ushered Howard into the foyer.

"Where is he?" Howard asked, sweating despite the chilly autumn evening. "I've got to see him now!"

"Of course, sir," the butler said; he's in the projection room. It's just been completed and I believe he's celebrating up there with a cocktail. I'll go up and tell him you're here."

"No, no need; I know the way."

"But, sir," the butler stammered as Howard raced past him toward the stairs. "He likes to be alerted when guests…"

Howard ignored him and hurried up the stairs, down the hall, and on to the attic. Earl was not to be found until Howard heard him call out from the small projection booth built in behind the bar.

"Come on back here, Howard."

Howard stood in the doorway of the room too small for two people and found Earl handling the reel on the projector. Earl was fumbling with the spools on the projector, a cigarette dangling from his lips. Without looking up at Howard he said, "Damned tape keeps freezing. I can't have that. It costs money to get these film prints. This tape gets stuck and the projector light will burn it up." He spun the receiving wheel to tighten the tape and then flipped the on switch. The screen at the opposite end of the room lit up. The picture moved along. "Maybe I fixed it."

"Earl, we've got to talk. Don't worry about the projector. There's more important..."

"What's more important? I've been planning this room for months. Now it better all be in working order or someone's going to be sorry." The film kept moving without pause.

Howard started to talk again but Earl, pleased with his repair job, patted his money man on the shoulder. "Howard, you get too riled up. Why don't you fix yourself a drink and then you can be the first visitor to see a dream come true?"

Howard followed Earl out of the projection room and stood behind the bar wiping sweat off his neck as Earl poured straight scotch into a glass and gulped it down. Earl led the way down the inclined floor to a front row seat and pointed for him to sit in the middle. Earl sat beside Howard, took a sip of his own scotch, stared at the screen, and said, "Capone's got nothing on me."

Finally Howard found his voice and said, "Earl, you can't stay here. You've got to get out of here, out of town, fast!"

"What the hell are you talking about?"

"I couldn't help it, Earl. I had to tell them. They threatened me. They would have killed me if I hadn't told them."

"Tell who what?" Earl demanded, squeezing his rocks glass so hard it broke in his hand.

"Artie and Murray, They had me picked up and taken to their office. They told me they knew something was wrong with the books. They said they knew you were skimming."

"How did they figure that?" Earl shouted. "You know how to fix the books. Hell, that's all you know how to do."

"It's this attic, Earl. They called it a luxury. They say you're living too high on the hog. I think they were guessing."

"So how did you straighten it out, Howard? What did you tell them?"

"What could I say, Earl? They kept saying, 'don't lie to us, Howard,' every time I opened my mouth. 'Don't want to hear any lies, boy. We don't like liars,' they kept saying. What could I do?"

"I hope you didn't do what I think you did," Earl said as he grabbed Howard's arm and squeezed.

Howard tried to move his arm but Earl's clutch was like a vice grip. "I couldn't help it," he said. "Don't you understand, Earl? They would've killed me. I had to tell them. They already seemed to know we'd been skimming. All I did was tell them what they already knew."

"Why you son of a..."

"No, Earl, don't be mad at me. I could have left town myself, but I didn't. You're my friend. I had to let you know. People are going to be coming for you. You've got to get out of town."

"So you're my friend," Earl said, his voice a low growl, "my good friend Howard; my good friend Howard the rat!" He squeezed Howard's arm tighter.

"Earl, you're not listening. I didn't have a choice but I had to let you know. You've got to get out of town. They're going to be coming for you. We can take whatever money you've got hidden here and leave town. We can go together."

"No," Earl said, his lips curling into a tight smile. "No, Howard, I don't have to go anywhere but into that room. I'll be fine."

"Room," Howard asked, "what room?"

Earl's smile widened, a menacing smile. He glanced toward the corner of the attic. "That room, Howard, that room over there. Oh, wait, that's right. You can't see the room, can you, Howard?"

"What are you talking about? What room?"

"Never mind, it doesn't matter to you, Howard, because it's true. You've got to go: only you, not me." Earl's hand jumped from Howard's arm to his neck and was joined by Earl's other hand, bloody from the broken rocks glass. Howard squirmed and tried to resist but he had nowhere near the strength of the barrel chested Earl. The choking cut off Howard's voice. It was over in two minutes. Howard slumped sideways in the front row seat.

Earl released his grip slowly and whispered,

"My old friend Howard, Howard the rat!" He got up from his seat, took out a handkerchief and wiped the blood from his hand. "Sorry you had to go alone, Howard, but don't worry about me. They won't find me. They won't find me, Howard. Nobody's going to find me."

He walked back to the bar, pulled a fresh rocks glass from the shelf with one hand and grabbed a full bottle of scotch with the other. He walked back down the incline. It was bittersweet to see that the projector was still working and the movie was still rolling. He just wanted to sit in the middle of his dream room and watch the chorus girls on the screen. There was no time for that now. He could hear yelling from down on the main floor of the house, loud voices calling his name. He waited and walked confidently to the corner of the attic. It wasn't what he saw that bothered him. It was what he didn't see. There was no light leading to a hidden hallway. There was no hallway, no door into a room that was so like the room that had reminded him of his mother. He dropped the scotch. The bottle shattered. "Mama," he called out, "Let me in. Let me in, Mama. Mama, please let me in. I'll be good. I won't disappoint you, Mama. Just please let me in!" There was silence except for voices coming from the second floor hallway. Earl threw the rocks glass against the only thing he could see, the corner of a room, nothing more. The glass shattered, splinters flew back at him. He felt frozen, felt nothing, no pain. He turned and saw Howard sitting very still. His old friend Howard, the only friend he ever had. He wished he could talk to Howard, wished he could talk to his old friend, but Howard ignored him. Who was Howard to ignore him? Howard was nobody. Howard was lucky Earl allowed him to be his friend. He told Howard exactly that as he moved toward the silent man, sat down beside him, started to talk, but didn't. Earl just looked up at the dancing girls on the screen, all the pretty girls in their tiny costumes and their long legs suddenly stopped in mid-air, a smoldering circle surrounding them, the screen smoking and then bursting into flame as Earl was rigid in his seat next to Howard, listening to footsteps on the stairs.

JIMMY AND
EFFIE - 1940

Jimmy Peters did not rush in to proposing to Effie Harwood in March of 1940. She was very attractive and thoroughly devoted to Jimmy, but she was the no-nonsense type who would not abide simply "playing around", something Jimmy had a history of enjoying. He really liked being with Effie but marriage would lead to some expectations that he actually do something to support a family and that, of course, would mean finding employment. Jimmy liked the minimal amount of work that he had to do to support his bachelor life. He only regretted not being financially able to work less.

They had been dating since the first of the year, having met at a New Year's Eve party, introduced by their respective dates. Jimmy had kissed his date at midnight, rushed to cut in on Effie's date, and broke up their lip-lock so that he, Jimmy, could show Effie what kissing's all about. Effie's date had angrily proceeded to separate the two and deliver a six-inch punch to Jimmy's right cheek followed in a split second by a hard slap to Jimmy's left cheek by Jimmy's date. The room had frozen in the middle of Auld Lang Syne until Jimmy, his hands patting both cheeks to make sure they were both there, broke out laughing, infecting Effie, then her date, then Jimmy's date until laughing and kissing spread throughout the room. Jimmy and Effie's date shook hands; Effie and Jimmy's dates hugged. All four switched partners and let auld acquaintance be forgot.

Jimmy had sexual hit and run on his mind when he and Effie necked out in the front seat of his sedan as the band played on inside the ballroom. His right hand was inching up her thigh at a consciously slow but steady pace and he was heading for home when she slapped her hand down on his, giggled, and said, "Slow down, sport. I like you but it's way too soon to decide how much."

The band stopped playing and so did Jimmy. He said, "I couldn't help myself; you're so beautiful." He once more slid the hand tentatively upward and she said, "Stop," even though she was still smiling.

He was no pouter and was pleasant, even jovial, as he drove her home. He was willing to see her again and she was willing to see him again. He was thinking, "One, maybe two dates and I'll have her." He quickly rethought that plan as they approached the guard gate at the entrance to the gated community full of mansions.

The darkness of night and his imagining the plans he had for Effie obscured his noticing the increasingly impressive houses to his right and left as they drove up to the top of the hill to her home. Three story brick homes with arches and porch columns and solariums and bay windows with two acre lots separating one house from the next dotted this wealthy section of the city's suburban west side. Since he had been lost in fantasizing about Effie, Jimmy had no idea that the sprawling edifice at the hill's summit dwarfed all the other impressive homes along the upward path. Had Jimmy been religious he might have used the word "epiphany" to describe the first thought that came to his mind as he gazed upon this contemporary castle: "Effie comes from money!" His plans for a hasty retreat after two or three dates were washed away. The girl was rich; she was a keeper, which is one of the reasons they were still together three months after New Years.

Jimmy had asked Effie more than once in that three months to meet her parents and more than once she had declined. He would say, "Isn't it time I met them?"

And she would say, "You're a gold digger."

"What's wrong with that?"

"Nothing if you're in the Klondike."

"You can't seriously think that I love you for your money."

"I think you love me because I'm beautiful, funny, intelligent, kind, affectionate, and because I have a lot of money."

"I'm not saying it makes you less attractive," he said one night at dinner, "but the only interest I'd have in marrying for money would be to use it to feed the hungry and clothe the poor."

"And how would you do that?" she asked.

"By taking my poor, hungry self to a fine, men's clothing store and then out for surf and turf."

"So is all this by way of a proposal?"

Jimmy choked on a bite of ham on rye that went down the wrong pipe and coughed until the question faded from memory. Reasonably certain that he would survive, Effie smiled and said, "I want dessert."

Jimmy met her parents the following night. His suit was blue serge under a brown felt fedora hat and a white linen scarf hanging over his lapels. All that was missing was the ascot. Though a butler opened the door for him, Effie was waiting to usher him in.

She commented on the white scarf. "What's that for? Are you cold?"

She was dressed in casual slacks and a cream colored blouse which he appraised sheepishly. "Did I overdress?"

She smiled, "Get rid of the scarf."

He tucked it into his pocket as she led him into a living room the size of half a football field, the walls covered with simply framed modern art and family pictures. The floor was dark wood; the coved ceiling, a circular staircase off the foyer led up to a second floor balcony. It was all impressive but not pretentious. It bespoke money without screaming it.

Jimmy stopped to gather it all in. He said, "This is really something!"

Effie turned to face him. "That's a bigger compliment than you gave me."

He put his hands on her shoulders at arm's length, looked her up and down, and said, "You are really something!"

"Oh you're sweet and so sincere."

"My sincerity is only rivaled by my humility. Most people tell me I'm great when it comes to humility."

"I'm sure they do."

She led him by the arm to the far corner of the room. They passed through the dining room with a table that could seat at least twenty.

"I didn't know you had such a big family."

"No, there's only Mom and Dad, Grandmother and I, but Grandmother weighs six hundred and fifty pounds and takes up sixteen chairs when we dine."

Well, she sounds like a crowd I'd like to meet."

"You can't. She's dead."

"Really? Jimmy raised an eyebrow. "What did she die of?"

"Malnutrition. Come on," Effie said, taking his arm. This isn't really where we eat. There's a breakfast nook in the kitchen. Let's go see if Mom's in there."

They passed through an alcove and down a short hallway, a wall of which was all windows looking out on a lavish garden with a beautiful array of colors, meticulously trimmed hedges, and walkways winding through the flowers. Jimmy almost stumbled as she led him along. He was unable to take his eyes off the multicolored spectacle. He righted himself as they walked into the kitchen.

Effie approached the two apron-clad women at the large enamel gas stove. Jimmy assumed they were servants until Effie said, "Hi, Mom; Hi, Nancy. I've got someone I want you to meet."

The woman called Nancy waited a while for the woman called Mom to lead the way as they walked across the expanse of kitchen. Mom reached out a hand to shake Jimmy's and said, "I'm happy to meet the man who so unabashedly wants to marry my daughter for her money."

Jimmy turned beet red. The other woman, Nancy, laughed. Effie tucked her arm through Jimmy's and said, "This is he, Mother. Jimmy Peters, this is my Mom, Darla, and this is Nancy, chef, major domo, and Mom's girl Friday."

Jimmy, still in mid-blush, stuttered, "H-hello; I-I'm, well, pleased to…"

"Oh relax, young man," Darla said, "Just my little joke. I'm sure there are lots of reasons you like

Effie. What's not to like? And which of her former suitors hasn't been interested in her money while pretending they're not?"

Then Nancy stepped forward, her round, chubby face all smiles as she shook Jimmy's hand. "Why don't you start earning your money by taking your best girl out to the vegetable garden to pick some more basil for dinner? We're having a nice Italian pasta dinner."

"Oh, lovely idea," said Darla, an attractive, older version of her daughter. "You wouldn't mind, would you?"

"No, not at all," Jimmy said, starting to fall in step with their strange sense of humor. "Now, will you be paying cash for my services, or should I bill you?"

Nancy laughed out loud. "Hah, bill us, please. We'll throw yours on the pile with all the others."

"And, Effie," Nancy added, "If you see your father out there, tell him it's time to shower for dinner."

"Yes," said, Darla, "He can go back to training for the Olympics tomorrow."

Effie, still holding on to Jimmy's arm led him across the kitchen through a small mud room and out the back door. He felt like he had just entered a botanical garden as they walked a path alongside the flowers, fragrances dancing in his nostrils. They crossed a small grassy square and moved toward another garden sprouting all manner of herbs. Suddenly someone yelled, "On your right!" It was a middle-aged man in sweat clothes and sneakers who raced past them, abruptly turned and ran around them three or four times, and stopped. "Hi ya, fella, I'm Effie's father, Lester. Call me Les. You obviously are Jimmy, unless Jimmy's already been dumped by my very popular daughter and replaced with you.

"No sir. I'm Jimmy." He shook the older man's hand. "To my knowledge, I haven't yet been dumped. He looked at Effie and asked, "Have I?"

She squeezed his arm, "Not yet, and Daddy, you stop teasing. I told you this one could be a keeper."

Les winked at Jimmy, "She'll be needing a keeper. Now, if you'll excuse me, I've got another ten minutes to run."

"Run where?" Jimmy asked.

"No where, anywhere, just run." Les pounded a palm against his heart. "My ticker's good. I want to keep it that way."

"Dad," Mom and Nancy want you to stop training for the Olympics and go wash up for dinner."

"Well, that's nice to hear," and off he ran directly away from the house. Then he turned abruptly and ran back to where Jimmy and Effie were standing. Les ran in place as he asked Jimmy, "By the way, you are planning to marry my daughter, aren't you."

Effie smiled. "He is but he doesn't know it yet."

"Why not?"

"I haven't told him."

Still running in place, Les said to Jimmy, "Oh well, maybe I jumped the gun, but when she does tell you to ask her to marry you, we can talk about your position in the firm. She told me you don't like to work and you're attracted to money. I'm sure we can find something to accommodate your interests or lack thereof." Les looked at Effie and said, "Like we did for Gary."

Jimmy's head jerked back and forth between Effie, apparently his future wife, and Les, evidently his future father-in-law. Highly confused, he simply asked, "Who's Gary?"

Effie said, "He's my uncle, Mom's brother, kind of lazy, very averse to work."

"Alright then," Les said with a tone of finality, "you'll make a lot of money with the firm. We'll talk after dinner over cognac and cigars. You smoke cigars?"

"I have, yes."

"Good, see you later," and off he ran.

Jimmy looked at Effie, hoping she could explain to him what had just happened. She said, "Let's go pick some basil."

Jimmy and Effie married in the fall of 1940, nine months after they met. The wedding took place in a very large, very old Episcopalian church to which neither of them belonged. Les, who made a tour of churches to find his favorite, had chosen this one for its sheer size and beauty. It sported large spires, raised brick, stained glass, angel-and-saint painted ceilings and master hand-crafted Stations of the Cross. Being agnostic, and his family having no affiliation with this church whatsoever, was not a problem once the pastor glanced at the size of the amount written on the check handed to him by Les as "a humble offering".

Jimmy, an orphan with no siblings, was going to invite some of his old, rough and ready friends until he calculated how many would tap him for handouts once they witnessed all the opulence. Besides, a lot of them were signing up for the military, part of the wave of patriotic fighting spirit spreading through the nation's young male population. Jimmy didn't share the enthusiastic desire to join up, much as he disliked the German joker named Hitler. As far as Jimmy was concerned, his old gang going off to Europe would be enough to flush the loud-mouth little German down the drain.

When he had discussed this with Effie some months earlier, she had said, "So you don't believe you'd be all that helpful if we should go to war over in Europe?"

"Can't see how," he assured her.

"So you'd just be in the way?"

"I believe so. I've never fired a weapon bigger than a sling shot. I'm not inclined to do much marching. I prefer a nice, soft mattress to an army cot. All in all, I'm just not a good fit."

She nodded after a second's consideration of his self-admitted deficits and said, "I see. You're willing to sacrifice serving your country to avoid being in the way."

"Exactly. Besides, when I start working for your dad after we're married, won't that be a form of service since his company makes a lot of money, pays a lot of taxes, boosts the gross national product, and reinforces that old adage, "He who works for his wife's rich father also serves?"

"Good thing the country's got you on its side."

"I agree, and anyway, we're not going to get into that conflict. This Hitler's a flash in the pan."

For a wedding present Les and Darla bought the young couple a house. This astounded Jimmy who wondered how many more strokes of luck could come his way. He listed an extremely likeable and beautiful wife, congenial and generous in-laws, the promise of a job that paid more in a year than he could ever expect to make in five years, a job-related draft deferment if needed, and now a house. As he and Effie stood looking at the three-story house plus basement for the first time, he told her, "Fate has decided that I should not be happy; I should be overjoyed." Then he picked her up and carried her to the front door.

She said, "Has fate also found a way for you to carry me across the threshold without having a front door key?" She then reached into her purse, pulled out the key and unlocked the door while still in his arms. He then did indeed carry her across the threshold, held her tighter and kissed her lips longer than the movie morals code would allow Clark Gable to kiss Carole Lombard.

He was about to carry her upstairs to the nearest bedroom when two things happened. He remembered there would be no bed until they bought one and someone came toward them from a room calling out, "Congratulations! Welcome to your new home."

"Les,' Jimmy called out with less than full enthusiasm, "and Darla, what a surprise!" He set Effie down and hoped his sexual ardor wasn't fully noticeable.

"Hi, Mom; Hi, Dad," Effie said and ran across the living room to hug them both. "I can't believe you're giving us such a beautiful house. This is so wonderful. I love you both so much. Thank you, thank you, thank you!"

"Why, sweetie, you're welcome," Darla said, "but we're just typical parents who want their daughter and son-in-law to be happy."

Jimmy, came up beside Effie while trying to recall any "typical parents" he knew of who bought homes for their kids. He shook hands with Les and hugged Darla. "By the way," he asked, "how did you get in?"

"Battering ram," Les said with a laugh. "No, we have a key to the back door. We didn't think you'd mind."

"Of course not," Effie said, "Our house is your house."

Jimmy, with some trepidation, could only agree.

Darla said, "So, you haven't seen the upstairs. I just know you're going to love it, especially the master bedroom. We had it furnished specifically to your tastes, Effie."

"Really, mom? Let's go see."

"Furnished?" Jimmy asked, startled. "It's already furnished?"

"Of course," said Les, "and what's more, the downstairs furniture will be delivered tomorrow. I hope that's not an inconvenience but, being newly-weds, we figured you'd want us to start with the master bedroom." He accompanied this with a slap on Jimmy's back and a lascivious little chuckle.

The master bedroom alternated light blue walls with white dresser, vanity, closet doors (two) and ceiling. The bed's headboard was rich mahogany and the bedspread was pink.

"Pink for girls," Darla said, "and blue for boys. You like?"

"We love it! Don't we love it, Jimmy?"

Squinting at the pink bedspread, Jimmy forced a smile and said, "What's not to love?"

Jimmy and Effie spent that night and much of the next day in the master bedroom. Making love and sipping champagne overrode any misgivings he may have had about the pink bedspread. It was certainly a shade he could live with given all his good fortune.

He was about to pour each of them another glass of champagne when the phone rang. He told Effie to ignore it but a second too late. "Oh, Cal, how are you? Did you enjoy the wedding? What a handsome best man. My friends all fell in love with you. In fact, there's one in particular I'd like you to meet. She's…, oh, really. I'll hand you to Jimmy."

Jimmy took the phone and said, "Hey, boy, how are you?"

"How am I?" answered the voice on the line. "I'm a nervous wreck. I've just enlisted."

"Enlisted? Enlisted in what?"

"What most people enlist in when they enlist, you dope, the military, the army to be specific."

Jimmy looked at Effie with an expression of what looked to her like mild shock and then he asked Cal, "Why would you do that?"

"Why? I've got a college degree and, after basic training and some additional training, I'll be a second lieutenant. That's why. It's a lot better than going in as a grunt."

"Sure, but whatever your rank, why would you enlist at all?"

"Why would I enlist?" Cal sounded confused. "Why does anyone enlist? To serve my country."

"But we're not at war."

"Jimmy, it's not hard to read the signs. Haven't you heard of lend-lease? We're supplying England with lots of weapons. When the guns go overseas, the manpower's pretty sure to follow."

"I think you're wrong, Cal. I don't believe it,"

Jimmy said, despite the uncertainty gnawing at his stomach. "It's not our fight over there."

"You've heard of Hitler, I presume," Cal said with some growing frustration. "That bastard wants to rule the world. He's got to be stopped."

"Let England stop him, and France."

"Are you serious? France can't resist him much longer and England's about to be going it alone. Our allies are under attack!"

There was a pause. Jimmy slid to a sitting position at the side of the bed. He softened his tone. "Cal, what you're doing is a bit scary isn't it?"

"Like I said, I'm a nervous wreck, but some things just need to be done. When you're dealing with guys like Hitler and that fat thug, Mussolini, it can't just be left to the other guy."

Another pause as Jimmy thought of new ways to challenge Cal's choice. "What about that college degree of yours, boy?" he finally asked. "You could probably be of more use to the USA if you put that to work in some way over here."

"Maybe, maybe not. All I know is my gut's telling me I should be ready to go over there. The reason I called you though, Jimmy, is that some of the guys are meeting at Hennessey's bar tomorrow night to give me a send-off. Could you be there?"

The conversation ended on a friendly note. Jimmy hung up the phone slowly and just as slowly glanced over at Effie who said, "So Cal's going in, isn't he?"

"Yeah, he is."

"Well," she said, getting out of bed and heading to the bathroom, "he's not alone."

Cal's party came and went. During the event a few others announced their decisions to enlist. Despite thinking them crazy, Jimmy said nothing since their announcements seemed to be met with overall approval. Jimmy had walked the few blocks from his house to Hennessey's bar and had not noticed the few posters hung on shop windows until the walk home. Uncle Sam was in full red, white, and blue regalia leaning forward and seemingly staring straight into Jimmy's eyes under the words, "I WANT YOU". Jimmy's mumbled response, "You can't have me," prompted a little chuckle. Or maybe it was the drinks he'd had at Hennessey's.

Effie was waiting up as he got home, reading a book in the living room. He greeted her from the foyer where he hung his overcoat and hat.

"How was it?" she asked.

"It was nice, nice to see the fellows. I felt bad for Cal."

"Why? Didn't anybody buy his drinks?"

Jimmy smiled. "Don't be silly. No, but, you know, enlisting and all. I just kind of felt sorry for him."

"I don't understand. This is his choice, isn't it?"

"Yeah," Jimmy agreed, sitting down on a chair near hers, but Cal can be impulsive."

"Unlike your thoughtful, restrained self."

Jimmy smiled again. "Okay, so I can be impulsive too but not impulsive enough to join the army." When she didn't respond, he asked, "Don't you think that's kind of a reckless decision?"

Her response was to set her book on the table between them, yawn, stretch, and say, "I think at a time like this everybody has to be guided by their own instincts and my instincts tell me it's time for bed." She tilted her head sideways to catch his eye and, in a whisper, asked, "Are you coming?"

Jimmy started working for Effie's father the following week. The headquarters of Les's domain took up the top three stories of a sky scraper in the central city. Jimmy walked through glass doors on the lowest of the three floors and entered a large reception area. He approached the semicircular desk where an attractive woman was juggling a bank of telephones. As she was finishing a call, he glanced at the pictures on the surrounding walls, mostly photographs of buildings representing various types of architectural styles. Then he turned back to the receptionist who was asking if she could help him.

Jimmy introduced himself and, without further explanation, he was acknowledged and told to wait while she rang Mr. Evans.

In half a minute a man walked toward Jimmy from one of the three hallways adjacent to the reception area. He approached Jimmy with a wide smile and a hand extended. "Gary Evans," he said,

"Les asked me to welcome you, Jimmy, and get you acclimated. Nice to meet you."

Jimmy shook hands and said, "My pleasure, Gary."

"So you're the lucky man who won Effie's heart. Great girl, Effie. Known her all her life."

"Really? So you've been with Les a long time."

"Ever since he married my sister. And by the way, sorry we weren't there at your wedding. We were vacationing in Europe."

Jimmy had a vague recollection of Les saying something about employing his brother-in-law. "So I guess that makes us family."

"It does and, believe me, it's a good family to be part of, I'm here to tell you. Let me ask you, Jimmy, did he buy you a house?"

"Well," Jimmy hesitated, "it was a wedding present."

So was ours, a wedding present. It sure beats a toaster, doesn't it? Hell, I say, 'Give me a house and I'll buy my own toaster.'" At this Gary laughed loudly, one big guttural guffaw, and then gave Jimmy a slap on the back. "Welcome to the family and welcome to the company and kiss all your worries away. Les'll treat you good and I should know."

"And what exactly do you do here, Gary?"

"Little as I can," this said with another guffaw. "Come on, I'll show you your office. It's down at the end of the hall, next to mine. That makes us neighbors. Les keeps me down here out of

47

harm's way. The real action's one and two floor's up."

"You mean the workings of the business? " Jimmy asked as they headed back down the corridor from which Gary had come. "What exactly are the workings of the business?"

"Damned if I know. Okay, I exaggerate. I know about the business. Les, as you probably know, is a developer."

"I do know that much. I'm just not all that clear about what's being developed."

"Houses, neighborhoods, buildings, industrial areas. Les builds cities so to speak, or grows cities. If it needs to be built, Les'll get it built."

They arrived at the end of the hall. "This one's mine," Gary said, pointing to the office on his left and then, pointing right, he added, "and this one's yours." Gary opened the door and stood to one side as Jimmy entered his office. It was small but not tiny. It being a corner office, a window looked uptown north and another looked east over the riverfront. In front of this east-facing window was a simple brown varnished desk and, across from the desk, two wing-back chairs. Along the south wall was a leather couch, also brown. He felt another pat on the back from Gary as the two stood in the doorway surveying the room. "Nice layout, huh, Jimmy?"

"Very nice, very very nice," Jimmy answered as he walked toward and behind the desk, swiveling the chair left and right, looking out one window and then the other. Finally he sat down in the chair and folded his hands on the desk. "So," he said to

Gary who was settled in one of the chairs, "what's my job? What do I do?"

"What do you do? Better not to ask. You start asking 'what do I do?' and the next thing you know, you might actually be asked to do something."

Jimmy shook his head in confusion. "I don't understand. I don't do anything? That doesn't make sense. So tell me, Gary, what do you do?"

"Me? I do the same as you but less of it. Then Gary glanced at his watch. "9:45," he said, "just about lunch time."

The days passed into a full week. On the second day of roaming the hallways, introducing himself to apparent coworkers assembled at the water fountains, staring north through one window and east through another, Jimmy had a visit from Les.

How ya doing, Jimmy?" he asked, "getting your sea legs?" He sat down in one of the wing back chairs. "Nice view of the river, don't you think?"

Jimmy agreed, "Yep, it's a great view. Les," he went on, "I really appreciate the job and this swell office, but I'm confused about my duties. Gary's been great but I haven't learned much about my job responsibilities."

"Oh, I see," said Les, "Well, all in good time, son. Now I've got to get back upstairs, but if you want something to occupy your time, go down to the reception area and ask for the company manual. It has a pretty extensive history of the company in it. Why don't you spend today reading that" Les stood up. "Tell you what, why don't you and Effie come by for dinner tonight? Darla and Nancy are working up a big steak and lobster dinner."

"Okay, sure," Jimmy said. "What should we bring?"

"Nothing. You just bring that daughter of mine. We'll provide the rest."

Jimmy read and re-read the company manual over the next five days. It wasn't in an effort to look for missed details on prior readings. There was just nothing else to do. He took it with him to the lunch room and read it there to give whoever might be watching the impression that he actually had something to do. One day in the lunch room, a man walked in and over to the announcement board upon which he thumbtacked a poster and then left. It was a poster of a grey bearded man with a no-nonsense expression, dressed in red, white, and blue tails and similarly colored top hat. His pointed finger and no-nonsense expression underwrote the seriousness of the caption which read, "I WANT YOU".

Jimmy stared back briefly, tugged at his starched shirt collar, then looked away. He looked back at the manual lying next to his coffee, then back at Uncle Sam. Viewing either felt uncomfortable and his shirt collar seemed to get tighter. He tugged at it again, gulped down the coffee and returned to his office.

He read the manual a few more times in his

office and then decided to visit Gary across the hall. Gary was just walking into his office as Jimmy crossed the hall. "Hey," Jimmy said, "What's up?"

"Gary hung his overcoat and hat on the coat tree inside his office door. "Just back from lunch," he said.

Jimmy had seen him leave for lunch at 11:30. Clock watching is inevitable when there's nothing else to do. It was now 2:45 and Gary went back into the hall.

"Where to now?" Jimmy asked.

Gary called back over his shoulder, "Coffee break."

A few hours later Jimmy closed his office door, headed to the elevator, went down the twenty floors of other disparate businesses and offices, and got off at the lobby. He noticed the poster board next to the cigar shop in the lobby. Once again Uncle Sam and Jimmy locked eyes. Jimmy hurried out the revolving door to the bus stop in front of the building. The same bus stopped at the corner of Jimmy's block so he travelled by bus happy to avoid fighting the traffic he'd encounter if he drove to work. He took a seat on the half full bus and leaned back for a relaxing ride home. He looked up at the advertising signs above the windows on each side. The first one he saw was Uncle Sam just staring.

Effie and Jimmy still felt a newlywed glow by their six month wedding anniversary. They dined that night at Antonio's Italian. It was not one of the tonier places Les and Darla had recommended. It was just a charming eatery in the basement of a downtown theatre. The wine list was good, the pasta was great, and chef/owner Anthony was fat, as any great Italian chef should be.

The two of them sat across from each other at a tiny corner table, digging into their heaping bowls of spaghetti. Effie asked, "Do you want to have a meatball fight?"

"Of course I do; who wouldn't? But then there'd be less to eat."

"Good point. I'll just have to settle for a pillow fight later on."

"I accept the challenge," Jimmy said, raising his wine glass

Effie clinked her glass to his. "Fine. The loser has to submit to all the other's secret desires."

Jimmy swallowed a bite of a meatball. "You've got secret desires?"

"Never mind. I'm more interested in learning what yours are on the off chance that I shall lose which, of course, I won't."

"The way the deal's set up, neither of us can really lose. It might take a little time from my beauty rest but it's not like I need to be fresh in the morning."

"Why not?" Effie asked, sucking a single noodle through rounded lips like a reverse whistle.

"Because at work, once again, they'll be nothing for me to do."

"But isn't that exactly what you want to do?"

She held his gaze with a curious expression that seemed to imply that Jimmy actually wanting to work was unimaginable.

"Well, yeah, I suppose that's every guy's dream, to ride the gravy train and make money just for being on the train. I just wonder when you'll start worrying that you married a bum."

"Why should I worry? I know I married a bum, but your overall good qualities compensate for your general sloth."

"Why thank you very much. You're too kind."

"I suppose I am. Anyway, the most important thing is that you're happy."

"I'm amazed that anyone could think that's the most important thing, but I think I could still be happy if Les gave me some kind of something to do."

"Oh, that reminds me," she said, "speaking of Daddy. He and Mom came by when you were out the other night and they helped me pick out colors for the basement."

"The basement?"

"Yes, the basement. You remember." Mother suggested it needs to be more than laundry room and storage space, and Daddy said his people could come in with an interior design plan and remodel the basement within a week. I'm so excited, I can't believe I forgot to tell you."

Jimmy picked at his pasta for a few seconds and felt heat spreading in his face. He shook his hand slightly to ward off a slow realization that this news made him angry despite knowing he should be grateful. He swallowed and looked up at Effie. "Boy, those parents of yours are something. They buy us the house, furnish it, and remodel the basement. What haven't they done to that place?"

"Well they haven't decided what to do about the attic."

"And they won't," Jimmy said to himself, "I will." He was amazed to consider how reactively these words popped into his mind. Fix up his own attic? What was he thinking? What a lot of work! What did he know about fixing up attics? Yet try as he may to ignore it, he knew that no one was going to touch that attic but him.

He said nothing more to Effie about this un-characteristic scheme. They just chatted and joked and grinned like young lovers as they sipped wine and chewed on meatballs. After coffee and a light dessert Jimmy walked up to the counter to pay his bill. As he stood at the register, pulling cash from his wallet, he glanced at the marker board listing the evening's specials and the poster taped to the bottom of the board. Sure enough, it was his Uncle Sam.

The attic had been an afterthought for Les and Darla when they purchased the house. Les had determined that it was structurally sound but in a messy condition. It could wait and be dealt with at some future time.

Jimmy had decided to make that time now as he climbed the staircase leading from the second floor hallway to the attic. He opened the door at the top of the stairs and peered into the darkness. He found the light switch and flipped it on. A ceiling lamp lit the large attic space, enough for him to survey his surroundings. The first and strangest thing he noted was the inclined floor slanting at about a thirty degree angle to the highpoint at the end of the attic farthest from him. The remnants of what might have been a service bar leaned against the same far wall, looking as if it had been attacked with a hatchet. Then he noticed what appeared to be theatre seats upturned and tossed against a side wall. He assumed they had been fastened to the metal brackets remaining in the slanted floor. The brackets were curved and bent as if the seats had been ripped away. All these broken things were riddled with holes. "Bullet holes," he thought to himself, recalling Les telling him about some gangster activity that was rumored to have gone on here back in the days of prohibition. He vowed to himself that any bad history would be a thing of the past. This room was going to be light, bright, and cheerful. This room was going to be for fun and play, fit for the children he and Effie talked about having "after a while". This room was going to be re-created and the work was going to be his, which was something he never imagined he would ever say to himself.

Weeks passed. Jimmy spent his days at work going around to different offices asking coworkers within if he could get them some coffee. He re-arranged his office furniture, restored his office furniture to its original arrangement, then rearranged it again. He asked the receptionist if he could spell her at the phones. No work was too humbling and he did not care how it looked to others. He was tired of doing nothing. Once he entered a large meeting room with hardwood floors being buffed by a janitor. Jimmy gave the janitor a break and completed the job himself.

The five o'clock bus ride home brought the welcome return to his wife and his real work, remodeling the attic. Sometimes Effie worked with him, offering advice or doing some lifting and hauling as he pulled up the boards of the angled floor and got rid of the theatre seats. She asked him several times how he, Jimmy Peters, perpetual man of leisure, could be so invested in this self-chosen work. She, for her part, never let on that she expected him to get tired of doing nothing. On the other hand, he did not want to sound ungrateful to or resentful of her exceedingly generous, if over-indulgent, father.

In time the detritus of the former theatre was hauled off and the empty attic with the new even floor was ready for painting, carpeting, ceiling repair, and furnishing. Even so, there was a long way to go. It would take most of the rest of 1941.

Jimmy had been working through the fall and the first few months of winter. He was not naturally handy and certainly unskilled in carpentry. He got books from the library from which he learned to hang ceiling, re-do flooring, patch up and spackle walls, install extra outlets. It was a long learning curve that caused it to be a long job. That was fine with him. He was feeling a pride in his accomplishments and doing things he would never have imagined himself doing. His enjoyment at the prospect of going to work every evening after returning from his so-called job was a complete surprise to him. It was with mixed emotions that he could see the end in sight as Thanksgiving passed.

There had been a big Thanksgiving feast at Les and Darla's house. Nancy the cook had outdone herself. The turkey was tender, the potatoes were buttery, and the steamed vegetables were seasoned to make even the most die-hard of vegetable haters ask for seconds. Cranberries, casseroles, hot rolls, all were perfect. The pumpkin pie could be had ala mode which is how Jimmy had his first and second portions with room still left for a small slice of mincemeat with coffee and cognac.

As Nancy entered from the kitchen to warm up the coffees, Les stood up and applauded her. The others joined in and room was made for her at the table. Nancy had eaten her dinner intermittently throughout the morning and early afternoon, tasting this and sampling that until she had tried some of everything she prepared. She was happy though to join the family with Les filling the coffee cup that Darla set before her and Effie pouring her a hefty snifter of cognac.

While everyone settled back into their places, Les began the holiday tradition. "Time for our thanks," he announced. "We've all got plenty to be thankful for so why don't I start by saying that, as always, I'm thankful for my wife, for my family, which includes you, Nancy, for this young fellow who seems to be making my daughter very happy, for the successful year the company's had, and for the fact that we live in this wonderful country."

He raised his glass. They all followed suit, said, "Here, here," and each sipped cognac. Then it was Darla's turn. "I'm grateful to be married to a man who allows me to live in a style to which I'm still not totally accustomed after all these years. I'm grateful for my daughter and for her husband who has become like a son, and I'm grateful for Nancy who knows what a bad cook I am, but who still lets me advise and consent like I know what I'm talking about."

Again everyone said, "Here here" and sipped cognac. Effie said, "I'm grateful for everyone at the table and for Jimmy especially because he shows me he loves me every day and because every day he makes me laugh." She said this as a tear formed and slid down her cheek.

Jimmy joined the others in the "Here here" and the sipping and then said, "I'm thankful to be here at this table with my wonderful wife and her parents who have always made me feel at home and Nancy who tries to make me fat with her excellent food. I'm grateful to you, Les, for giving me a job and

I hope someday I'll be able to show you it was a good decision."

Another round of "here, here" and more sipping as Nancy said, "I'm grateful that we've managed to stay out of this war overseas and pray for all the boys getting ready to go if we're drawn in, especially my favorite nephew Billy who enlisted yesterday. God Bless 'em all." Her voice broke but she choked out the words. The "here, here" was more subdued and a thoughtful silence briefly held sway at the thought of the foreign war that threatened to slowly draw in the United States. Jimmy broke the silence by excusing himself to use the bathroom. He didn't need to use the bathroom; he just needed a moment to himself, a moment to clear his head. His head, however, was clear, all except for that recurring image of Uncle Sam.

Jimmy worked feverishly with the attic's finishing touches: dropping the last of the ceiling and some touch-up plastering and repainting. The furniture was delivered and arranged tentatively with matching floor lamps, two chairs, and a love seat with smaller table lamps on end tables. Nearly two weeks had passed since Thanksgiving. Jimmy should have been excited about the completion of his project but he remained preoccupied with the image of Nancy's nephew enlisting. He also had ongoing thoughts of his friend, Cal, and now other friends and acquaintances, all signing up for the war that was all but inevitable.

He tried to shrug it off. He thought of calling down to Effie to show her the finished product but, somehow, nothing felt finished. He stood in the center of the room and surveyed what he had done. He had done well. He should have felt proud. He had never worked on anything this persistently in all his life. The job Les had given him that required him to do nothing had become increasingly oppressive. Any time he asked Les for some kind of meaningful work, Les always said the same thing, "Forget about it, son; work's not for you. Besides, your job is to keep my little girl happy." This paradise he had fallen into felt daily more hellish. He felt daily more useless.

He did keep Effie happy though, never letting her know how much he hated the job. They steadily bantered, joked, dined out, and made love. He decided he should forget about the job and the foreign war. "After all," he told himself, "Christmas is around the corner." It was, in fact, December 6, 1941 when he noticed something he had not seen in all the months he had been in the attic. Despite none of the new lights being turned on or even plugged in, he saw dim illumination coming from the corner of the attic near the front window. To his amazement, then, he saw a hallway.

Bemused, confused, and wondering if he were hallucinating, he eased over warily to the corner. For the first time he saw the short hallway, the door at its end, and the light coming through the transom above the door. He opened it cautiously and stepped into a room that was dimly lit. He paid no attention to how it was furnished, the color of the walls or the curtains over the windows. All of that faded into distant consciousness. His entire focus was on the man standing before him. "Uncle Sam?" he asked.

"Who else would dress this way?"

Jimmy considered this, despite his disoriented state, and said, "Maybe a barker in a carnival."

"Maybe, but did you see posters all over town advertising a carnival?"

"No."

"Of course not. You saw me, Uncle Sam, pointing my finger at you, Jimmy Peters."

"Why?"

"Why? You ask why? Didn't you read the posters? Why else? Because I want you!"

"But I thought that meant everybody. That you want, well, I mean, every able-bodied young man."

"Every individual, able-bodied young man, that's right. Now tell me, Jimmy, are you an able-bodied young man?"

"I believe so, Uncle. In fact, I can show you a job I just finished right outside that door that...," Jimmy paused, ..."that door I never saw before. Oh my God! I've gone crazy!"

"You're ignoring my questions. You say you're an able-bodied young man. Are you an individual?"

"I think I am, yes, but…"

"No buts. You're the individual, able-bodied young man who I want."

"So, you're drafting me?"

"How can I draft you, Jimmy Peters? As far as either of us know, I'm just an hallucination. I may be just your mind telling you something."

"Telling me what?"

"Telling you to enlist."

Jimmy asked his Uncle Sam if he, Jimmy, could sit down. "I'm just kind of thrown off balance by all this," he added as he sat in a chair next to where Uncle Sam stood. "To tell you the truth, I've been thinking about enlisting, but, you know, we haven't even entered the war and…"

Uncle Sam held up a hand to interrupt him. He leaned over to Jimmy's side and turned on a radio on Jimmy's right. Jimmy heard the voice of a man who sounded like the President saying, "This day shall live in infamy" and "We have nothing to fear but fear itself."

Jimmy looked up at his uncle who switched off the radio and said, "It looks to me like you haven't yet heard about what happened today at our naval base in Pearl Harbor."

The room went dark. Jimmy found himself standing in the corner of the attic. No hallway, no door, no light, but he didn't doubt the truth of his experience, not for a minute. He walked to the attic door and down the two flights of stairs to the living room. Not surprisingly, given the frequency of their visits, Les and Darla were in the living room having cocktails with Effie. Jimmy approached them and looked at Effie. He said, "I have something to tell you."

"Effie looked alarmed. "What is it, Jimmy?"

"I have something I feel like I have to do."

"I know, darling. I know you're going to enlist." She stood up and hugged him, smiling through tears. "I know you have to. I've known for a long time the kind of man you are."

Les and Darla rose and walked to Jimmy and Effie. Darla gave Jimmy a hug as soon as Effie released him. Les said, "Your job will be waiting for you when you get back."

Jimmy shook Les's hand. "That's kind of you, Les, really kind, but I'm going to have to talk it over with Effie before I make that choice. You see, I think I need to find out something about what I'm good for, something I have to offer, something that I'm supposed to do."

Now Effie hugged him again. "Of course you will," she said, "and I'll be right there with you. Now go, darling, and do what you have to do."

He embraced her one last time, moved toward the door, and, after a final wave, left the house. The three of them waited until he was gone for Effie and Darla to break into tears. Les threw his arms around them both. They stood there in a three-way embrace until Effie was able to move away and wipe her eyes with her handkerchief. "I knew you'd both find out what I've believed all along. I knew he was more than some loafer happy to live off his wife's money."

"You know we hoped you were right," Darla said, "We just weren't sure."

"Effie, I knew he was alright when he started bringing his coworkers coffee and buffing the floors. That brother-in-law of mine, Gary, there's a loafer for you. He never gets edgy or feels any shame taking money for doing nothing. I couldn't imagine him answering phone calls so the receptionist could have a break."

"So you no longer think I made a mistake, Dad?"

"I know you love him and that's all that's ever mattered to me. I'd have supported the two of you same as I support Gary and your aunt. But now I know that that young man's alright, Effie. Yes sir, that Jimmy Peters is alright."

Tears formed in Effie's eyes again as she said, "I just hope he'll be alright."

Effie tried to keep busy after Jimmy's enlistment. They wrote every day of his basic training. He assured her that he would single-handedly beat the Nazis and return home with the Congressional Medal of Honor in time to declare his candidacy for president of the United States. She would laugh through tears falling onto his letter, blurring the ink.

One day when she was particularly lonely

after several hours of volunteering to help organize a local USO, she returned home, hung up her coat in the foyer, bypassed the living room, and started up the staircase. Then she opened the door to the attic as if she were being drawn up there. Jimmy had put so much of himself into restoring the attic that she had trouble spending time up there. It heightened her sense of his absence. Today, though, she felt she had to be in the attic, that she had to be in this part of the house that Jimmy had made his own.

When she arrived at the top of the second floor, she felt a slight chill. The vents had been closed and heat from the rest of the house had been limited. She turned on the light switch and walked into the room. The wall hangings, prints of nature scenes, landscapes, and ocean sides were comforting, but the loneliness and sadness still felt oppressive as she sat down in one of the easy chairs. She broke into tears as she said out loud, "Oh, Jimmy, it's a beautiful room. I just wish you were here."

As she wiped the tears away and took a deep breath to calm herself, she glanced over to the corner of the attic where a dim light was shining. She could not understand where it came from and walked over to investigate. Then she saw the hallway that shouldn't be there and the door beneath the transom. She asked herself, "What's going on?" She walked to the door as if being gently pulled forward. She opened the door and walked into a brightly lit room with sunlight streaming through the windows. The day had been cloudy and chilly but this room was warm with a feeling of spring about it. The furnishing had flower-printed upholstery. The walls were white with clean, fresh paint. Her mood suddenly took on the enthusiasm and joy of the first sunny, blue sky day after a wintry month of Sundays. She had no idea how this room could have concealed itself from her, her mom, and dad, and, presumably, Jimmy. Jimmy had never mentioned it to her in all the time he had worked on the attic. Yet, she didn't feel the need to question or doubt or believe she was going mad; she accepted the room's being there as something that was right and necessary, something that had to be present when its presence was needed. Real, unreal, fantasy, magic, illusion, it didn't matter. Here it was and here she was, filled with spirits that were lifted up with hope and courage and certainty that all was as it should be and that all would be well.

ERNIE AND
FRANKIE - 1961

She went by the name Ernie though her mother complained that she wasn't baptized Ernestine to wind up with a nickname that made her sound like a cigar smoking plumber. But the young woman felt comfortable being Ernie and idiotic being Ernestine. Not yet thirty, she was old in the eyes of her mother who would often warn Ernie that unmarried at thirty equaled spinster. Mom played fast and loose with math. Ernie ignored her, loved her, put up with her and took care of her until the old lady died. Ernie was left a tidy sum that allowed her to quit her job in a secretarial pool which provided a minimal income and occasional gropes and pinches from the group of middle managers, all male, for whom Ernie and the other female secretaries typed. She wanted to go back to school eventually, having left college in her junior year to care for her mother whose health had begun its decline. Ernie wanted out of the cheap, little apartment she and mom had shared. Pinching pennies was one of the reasons Mom could leave Ernie a small fortune.

Ernie had no siblings. At nine years old, frightened and confused, she asked her mom, strictly against her dad's directives, why dad still insisted on helping Ernie bathe. Dad was gone that afternoon, never to be seen again. Ernie did have cousins, Cousin Effie being her favorite and the woman Ernie most admired. Effie had been left a considerable fortune by her parents and she spent a lot of time overseas working on behalf of UNICEF. Consequently, one of Effie's houses was empty and offered to Ernie for as long as she needed a place to stay. Effie couldn't promise Ernie that she would always have the house to herself given that other family members stayed there for various reasons and for short periods of time while Effie travelled.

Ernie had been living in the house only a few weeks by the time she answered Frankie's knock on the door. The 19 year old standing before her on the front porch bore only the vaguest resemblance to the toddler for whom she babysat so many years earlier. Their common link was the marriage between her aunt Darla and his uncle Les, cousin Effie's late parents. Ernie was always confused about levels of cousinhood and, in this case, Les and Darla were uncle and aunt to both of them by marriage, but not by blood.

"Hi, Ernestine," he said in a quiet voice and his facial expression was somewhere between shy and expectant. The expression was hard to read. She hoped he wasn't like so many teenagers seemed to her, deadpan and sullen. She didn't want to be forcing conversation with a slug.

"Call me Ernie," she told him as she stepped aside and motioned for him to come in.

"Ernie?" He raised an eyebrow.

"That's what I go by." She looked him over head to toe and said, "You've grown, Frankie."

"People do," was all he said. He stood in the foyer and glanced into the large living room. "I haven't been here for years."

"Yes, when Effie wrote me that you were coming, she mentioned that she hadn't seen you for a while. Well, drop your duffle bag down and come on in. Oh, you can hang your coat in the closet."

He did so and then followed her into the living room. After she sat down on the couch, he sat across from her in a wing-back chair. "I hate to sound like a beggar, but I haven't eaten all day. Any chance I could make myself a sandwich?" He asked.

"Oh, sure, come on. I'll show you the kitchen.

"No need to," he said, getting up and walking across the room, "I remember where it is." Then he stopped and looked at her shyly. "I've got money; I can pay for what I eat."

She pursed her lips together and shook her head back and forth. "Don't be silly. Go fix yourself whatever you want. Since it seems we're going to be roommates for a while, we can figure all that out later. Actually, I could use a cup of coffee." She got up and accompanied him into the kitchen.

When they got there he seemed to have a homing instinct on where to find bread, cheese, and pressed ham. She watched as he assembled his sandwich. He wore black jeans, black sweater and loafers, and, of all things, a black beret. She was aware of the beatnik movement emerging out west in San Francisco. "I hear you write poetry," she said.

"Who told you that?"

"Apparently your dad told Cousin Effie who told me."

"My dad." He almost spit the two words and then he shook his head. His dad was Effie's uncle, Effie's dad's brother-in-law. He worked for Uncle Les until he retired. Frankie never was clear about why. He only knew that his retired father started hanging around the house all day, drinking beer and watching game shows on T.V. and that the house was less and less livable as time went by. He moved in with friends and lived off a generous allowance provided by his mother until dad told her to stop. "If he wants to live on his own, he can pay his own way," Frankie heard his dad tell her once when Frankie came to collect his allowance. She gave it to him, hugged him, begged him to move back home, and said, "You're dad insists there's to be no more money." Frankie left speechless. The laziest man in the world was insisting Frankie pay his own way.

He became aware of his own sullen mood. He

forced a smile to the best of his ability as he finished assembling his sandwich. Ernie was sitting with her fresh cup of coffee at the small breakfast nook table that looked out over the back yard. He joined her with his sandwich and a glass of water. "I remember you from when I was really little. You use to babysit for me."

"I did, and you could be a handful."

Now, with a more relaxed smile, he said, "Probably still am."

"So, you're a poet."

"Not really, since I'm not published but, yeah, I write poetry."

She sipped her coffee, giving him another appraising look over the rim of the cup. "Do you try to get published?"

He nodded with a mouth full of ham and cheese. "Yeah, I send things out. No luck so far." His face lit up to reveal some of the innocence of the little boy she recalled. "I read my stuff though and some people seem to think it's pretty good."

"Really? Where does this happen?"

"Place where I work sometimes, a little coffee shop down near the campus called 'The Dungeon'. Cool place. Some people play guitars, some, like me, read their poems."

"You work there? You mean you get paid for reading your poems?"

"No, I get paid for working the counter, washing the dishes, and sweeping the floor." He grinned. "I throw in the poems for free."

"You mentioned the campus. Are you going to school?"

"No. I went for a few years but my grades weren't great. My dad said that if I didn't end the final semester on the Dean's List, he'd stop paying, and I didn't, and he did." Frankie lowered his eyes and then looked out the window at the back yard before turning back to Ernie. "So, what about you? What have you been up to since I needed to be baby sat?"

Now holding her coffee cup at chin level with two hands, she shook her head, smiled, and said "Nothing as interesting as writing poems. There's actually some similarities in our stories. I'm just recently living on my own too."

"Divorced?" he asked with more curiosity that concern.

She smiled and her face reddened slightly. "No, no, never married."

"Really? You? Why not? I mean...," his voice faltered as he sensed the insensitivity of the question, "I mean, even as a kid I remember thinking you were really pretty."

Now she laughed out loud. "And now you see this haggard old maid sitting here."

"No, I didn't mean that. What I meant was, I don't know." He hesitated. "I mean you're still really pretty. I would think a lot of men would...." He stopped and wiped his hand across his face. He turned his eyes from hers and his face turned a deeper shade of red than hers. "I can't believe what stupid stuff I'm saying."

"Not at all, Frankie, you're sweet. Thanks for the compliment. I have had some offers but, you see, I had some responsibilities that got in the way."

"What responsibilities?" he automatically asked and, again checking himself, added, "If it's not too personal."

"No it's fine. It's my mom. She's needed a lot of care these past few years. I was the only one she'd let take care of her. It was a full time task. Everything else took a back seat."

He nodded, not fully understanding. "I don't know if I could do that, be that unselfish, especially with my dad." He thought about it through a bite of his sandwich. "Maybe with my mom."

"I haven't seen your parents since you were a child but I remember her as being very sweet. I don't remember your dad as well. Isn't his name Gary?"

"Yeah, Gary."

"I remember him driving me home from babysitting you a few times but I can't recall him well."

"He's pretty forgettable but never mind about him. What are your plans now that your mom is gone? Think you'll get married now?"

She tilted her head as she paused to study him with an appraising stare. "You know, Frankie, it's funny. Based on your black outfit and the fact that you write poetry, I'd think you might have some things in common with those west coast beatniks."

"Oh, yeah," he answered almost reverently, "Kerouac, Corso, Ginsberg, I love all that stuff."

"So isn't it a little bit of an old-fashioned, middle-class attitude to assume that all a single woman wants is to be married?"

His jaw dropped just prior to finishing off the sandwich. This cousin of his was no slouch. She was pretty hip to what's been happening in the world. "I guess you're right. Why does everyone think they need to be married? There are a lot of things a single woman can do with her life without being married, or a single man. Maybe marriage is becoming a thing of the past."

She shook her head. "I don't think so, but I do think it's not for everyone." Wanting to end a vague feeling of discomfort as they talked about marriage, she asked, "Can I read some of your poems?"

"If you want, sure. Let me go get my notebook. It's still in my duffel bag."

They returned to the living room. He got the notebook from his bag in the foyer and sat down next to her on the couch. He flipped open the notebook and glanced through a few pages until he found the one he wanted. He looked up and asked. "Do you want me to read it?"

"Please."

He cleared his throat and leaned forward over the poem. "It's called 'The Alley'."

It winds like a snake through the city
Streaked with debris and tripping
Over cracked and chunked concrete

Where garbage smells assault the senses
And stumbling bodies crawl
Can to can, seeking treasures
Of discarded food tossed out
The back of restaurants
Where the wealthy fatten themselves
On overpriced food and wine,
Cozy and safe from scavengers
Hunting the alley for leftovers,
Old fruit and bread crumbs discarded
To nourish the ghosts of the alley.

He looked up expectantly awaiting the praise he anticipated. When she remained silent, her eyes cast down, he asked, "Well, what do you think?"

She looked up, her expression thoughtful, curious. "Do you spend a lot of time in alleys?"

"Do I spend a lot of time in alleys? No, not a lot, but that's not important. You see, it's kind of what you might call a protest poem. In a way, the alley is a metaphor. It represents the bigger picture, the world at large."

She nodded agreement. "No, I understand that, but before it's any of that, it's first and foremost an alley, a street that runs behind houses and buildings. Before the words of a poem become metaphors or similes or 'the world at large', they are just what they are."

Now Frankie looked down, crestfallen. "So, you didn't like it."

"I didn't say that. You clearly have a feel for

poetry and a way with words. But somehow, even though I haven't seen you for years, I have a feeling there's a separation between the young man sitting across from me and the subject matter of your poem."

So I have to live in an alley before I can write about one?"

"No, you could just glance down an alley, even a filthy alley like the one in your poem, and notice some things that come out of a moment, out of a single piece of broken glass. It could be something like, oh, I don't know, a tossed away wad of aluminum foil next to a garbage can that sparkles like a diamond when hit by the sun. It's still a piece of discarded junk amidst the garbage but, in that moment, you see something beautiful."

He pressed his lips together and tilted his head. "Huh, I guess I never thought of that. You know, you're pretty good with words yourself. Maybe you should write poems."

"Oh, I do," she said and then stopped abruptly as if trying to erase the words.

"So, when you said you didn't write poetry you were holding out on me. Can I see some?"

"Oh. No, Frankie. I'm sorry. They're... well, they're very personal. They're just me trying to work out things in my own mind. They stay locked up in a journal, not for public consumption."

"Nobody ever gets to read them?" His ingratiating smile was his plea for an exception to be made in his case.

"No, nobody." She felt his disappointment and assumed that he judged it unfair for her not to be responding in kind after he had read his poem to her. "You're the one who's pursuing a poet's life," she assured him. "You should keep at it until you find the voice that's absolutely your voice and no one else's."

Now his smile broadened in response to what felt like a compliment despite the element of critique informing him that he had not yet found his voice. To say more about his poetry and hers felt awkward at this point. He simply said, "Thanks for the sandwich." He stretched and yawned then and asked, "Where do I sleep?"

"Oh, of course, you probably want to get settled in. There's actually three bedrooms in addition to the one I'm using upstairs, but there's also an attic that Effie had converted into a kind of little apartment with a bathroom. You might like it up there. It's a perfect place to write."

"Sounds good to me," he said. I'll just grab my bag."

Ernie sat up in bed making some notes in her journal. "Frankie, nice kid, trying to find himself, trying to be a beatnik. Writes poems about things he hasn't experienced. Tries to be moody and sullen like a good beatnik but he smiles like the middle-class, well-fed, pseudo rebel that he is. He's likeable. He can't stand his father, Gary. Can't blame him. When I baby sat for Frankie his dad would drive me home and flirt with me. I was fifteen or six-teen. Once he put his hand on my leg and he yelled "shit!" when I slammed my fist down on it. Family lore has it that Effie's dad employed him only so the old man's sister, Gary's wife, wouldn't have to work. Gary was, also according to family lore, a total dead beat. Now he's retired. My guess is he was put out to pasture with a pension to get rid of him. Right kind of dad to run away from."

She was about to put the notebook down, turn off the table lamp beside her bed, and go to sleep, but, flipping through some of the pages, she landed on one of her poems called "Ella":

Where are you now,
Wrapped in silk,
Breast pressed against the fabric?
What finger caresses the nipple
As your moaning whispers
Between your too red lips?
Who is she, tongue locked
To your thigh, tasting your moisture?
When the heat explodes
And you lie back panting,
Rolling over, your back to her,
Do you think of me?
Do you feel my touch
Against your nakedness
Or have I vanished
Like the last deep scream
Of passion before the silence?

She thought of Ella, trying to recapture the

feel of her in beds they shared in hidden places out on highways, checking into separate motel rooms where no one would see them sneaking down hallways.

Frankie was in the attic apartment very comfortable in an overstuffed chair, trying to read a book but distracted by thoughts of his distant cousin, Ernie. Ernie who writes poems and knows about beatniks and who is really pretty; he never knew he had such a sharp cousin. He started calculating how distant a cousin she was.

With Ernie not currently employed and Frankie only working part time, they seemed naturally to fall in together and establish a mutually agreeable companionship. She took him to lunch at her favorite diner. He took her to an old neighborhood theatre that showed only foreign and art films. They traded books of poetry; they toured the art museums together; they stayed home some nights and watched TV. Their ease with each other was at a level where shared silences were not uncomfortable. As they took in the autumn colors, walking through a large city park, he broke the silence and asked, "How does it happen that a girl who looks like you hasn't been snatched up by some lucky guy?"

She continued to stare up at the red leaves falling from the trees clustered along the path they walked along. "Snatched up?" she repeated, smiling, "Like in a butterfly net or like some lassoed horse?

I don't know if snatched up sounds all that good to me."

"You know what I mean." He hesitated but she said nothing. He glanced at her shoulder length brunette hair turning light red as it caught the sun. He could feel his heart beating at the sight of it. Despite her reserve, he wanted to test the waters, to get closer, and he found himself saying, "I only ask because you are really beautiful."

"No I'm not," she answered abruptly, picking up her pace.

It surprised him. He wanted to assure her that she was wrong, that she really was good looking but something felt wrong about pressing the issue. He simply said, "Sorry, I didn't mean to get too personal."

His embarrassment grew through another twenty seconds of silence until, curving along the path, they came to a clearing beyond which a stand of trees glowed golden, orange, yellow, and red beneath a deep blue sky through which pillows of pure white clouds lazily floated along. At last she spoke. "Now that," she said, "is really beautiful."

After a month of cohabiting, Ernie and Frankie fell into a rhythm. Frankie who had a history of shirking housekeeping responsibilities, perhaps reactive to his dad's general sloth, became an equal partner in household cleanup. He washed dishes, vacuumed carpets, raked leaves, cooked from his limited repertoire of dishes, and generally kept an eye on what needed to be done.

Ernie, who had not looked forward to sharing a house with Frankie when Effie asked if it would be alright, had come to thoroughly enjoy his presence and had trouble imagining being in the place without him.

She surprised him one night when he was working his part-time job at the coffee shop. He had been alternating working the counter and washing dishes. He was about to take a break and walk to the stool and microphone in the corner where the regulars and occasional newcomers read their poems. As he sat on the stool and riffled through his sheaf of poems, he looked across the room and saw Ernie walk in. Delighted at the timing of her entrance, he called out to the waitress roaming the tables, "Hey, Iris, that's my cousin at the door, take good care of her, will you?"

Iris, whose general expression was somewhere between flat and scowling, looked at Frankie as if she were about to tell him to go to hell. Then she glanced at the woman coming in from the front door and down the three steps into the room full of tables and booths. Iris broke into an uncharacteristic smile which Frankie feared might crack her face like old plaster. "Sure, Frankie," she said, "I'll take good care of your cousin."

Frankie waved and smiled at Ernie as Iris found her a seat in a corner table set up for two. Unusually chatty and accommodating, Iris took Ernie's order as Frankie found the new poem that

Ernie had inspired.

He spoke clearly into the mike. "Someone who knows about poetry told me I should write about what I know. I'd like to dedicate this one to her." He cleared his throat and said, "This one's called 'Dirty Dishes'." There was laughter in the audience as he began:

> Melted cheese congealed
> Like settled tar, stuck
> Next to dried egg yoke
> Makes me crazy,
> Makes me curse
> Cheese omelets
> And all those who order
> But leave remnants
> As if someone
> On the receiving end
> Of their bussed plates
> Weren't left to do battle
> With uneaten morsels
> that would have done what
> had they been eaten?
> Caused instant obesity,
> Indigestion, nightmares
> And troubled sleep?
> No, these last mouthfuls
> Mean no harm
> Offer nourishment
> And are, in fact, our friends
> That become my nightmares,
> Enemies to me who rubs

And scrapes and saws
Through concrete food waste
That calls to mind
The golden rule of mothers
Around the world:
'don't leave the table
Till you've cleaned your plate.'

This was met with laughter and applause beyond the approval he had ever gotten from writing about dirty alleys. He looked at Ernie across the room. She was clapping and smiling and gave two thumbs up that sent chills up his spine.

He exited the makeshift stage area and crossed the room to Ernie's table. Iris was coming from another direction to refill Ernie's cup but her friendly expression returned to its normal sourness as she watched Frankie sit down. "Aren't you supposed to be working?"

"Yes, Iris," he answered, "and right now I'm taking a two minute break to talk to my cousin."

"Well, I guess I can't blame you." The smile returned and Iris refilled Ernie's cup. "Anything else I can do for you, hon?" She accompanied this with a wink.

Ernie shook her head. "I think the coffee will do it for me."

"Okay, but you just wave if you need anything."

As Iris returned to the counter, Frankie whispered, "You gotta watch out for that one; she's kind of strange if you know what I mean."

Ernie expressed curiosity with a tilt of her head and a half smile. "No, what do you mean?"

"Um, okay, the word is, she doesn't like men."

"Well, you know, Frankie, some men can be pretty obtuse."

"No, I don't mean she doesn't like some men."

"I know what you mean. I wasn't born yesterday. Does her not liking men bother you?"

"No, of course not; why should it bother me? I have no interest in her. Why should I care?"

Ernie sipped some coffee and put down the cup. "So, let me understand. It would only be important if you were attracted to her?"

He thought for a moment, feeling uncomfortable in the face of what looked like a challenge. "I just think that if I were attracted to someone who liked women, you know, in that way, that I certainly wouldn't stay attracted because that would be way too weird for me." He shook his head back and forth as if he had just swallowed a bad oyster. "Anyway, I do have to get back to work but I just came over to say thanks for coming. I'm open to any more advice you can give me about poetry." He got up and walked to the dish room.

Ernie slumped into her chair as he left her there. When she saw Iris approaching with the coffee pot, she waved her away, set a five dollar bill on the table, picked up her coat and purse and headed for the exit.

The housemates grew closer over the next

few weeks. They took turns cooking, watched T.V., went to some movies, and talked about poetry. Ernie volunteered at a local Red Cross chapter one night a week and audited a music appreciation class at a local college on another night. Frankie felt a little down and a little lonely on these nights in the same way that she felt on the nights when he worked at the coffee shop that didn't coincide with her nights out. They generally waited up for each other, often with a cup of hot chocolate or a glass of wine to offer when the other arrived. He would ask her about her class or about some crisis to which she had responded along with her team of Red Cross volunteers. He would report favorable or less than favorable audience response to the poems he read on his break and they would analyze why one poem worked better that another.

One night he surprised her by saying, "I've been thinking about going back to school."

"Really? What brought this about?"

"You don't think I should?"

She shook her head and said, "Of course you should if you know what you want to do."

He smiled and stared into his hot chocolate. "That's just it. I really don't know. Also, I like working at the joint and reading my poems and," he looked up shyly, "living here." He was about to add, "with you," but was too embarrassed.

"So how would school interfere with that?"

"I don't know. I guess it wouldn't right away, but things change. Aunt Effie won't be gone forever and you, you'll find some guy eventually and move on."

She laughed. "Not any time soon," she answered emphatically.

He waited for her to say more, unclear as to why not any time soon. She just yawned and stretched and said, "This hot chocolate's making me drowsy. I think I'll turn in. Can you get the lights when you come up?"

He sipped the rest of his hot chocolate still baffled by her abrupt response. After a while he turned off the downstairs lights and went up to the attic to do some writing.

Life was moving along at a relaxed and uneventful clip in the home shared by the two cousins. He showed her some new poems. The feedback was positive. One afternoon he came home while she was vacuuming. She didn't hear him enter and he called out to her for a second time before she shut down the Hoover. "What is it?" she asked, alarmed. "Has something happened?"

"Something did, something great and very scary. I'm going to be the featured poet Saturday night at the coffee shop. It won't just be a walk-on on open stage night. I'm the featured poet on the busiest night of the week."

She brushed strands of hair from her eyes and clapped her hands together. "How wonderful, Frankie. That's just great!"

"Yeah, unbelievable." He walked from the

foyer to the living room and flopped in a chair. "Apparently people like the new stuff I've been writing: crazy stuff about washing dishes and being a college dropout, and being a middle class kid pretending to be a suffering poet. It's all working, just like you said."

She laughed. "What did I say?"

"You said I should write what I know about and you implied I was taking myself too seriously. Now that I've thrown some humor into my mundane life, people want to hear more."

"Frankie, I'm so happy for you."

He looked up shyly. "It would be great if you could come."

"Of course I'll come. I wouldn't miss it."

She was there and, along with a full house of others, she was hanging on every word, laughing at the right places, joining heartily in the appreciative applause. Frankie was a hit. She felt as proud of him as would be a teacher whose best student is accepted at Yale. She could hear elements of their kitchen table conversations and that he was writing from his own experiences and finding his voice. She could tell that that was an ongoing process still unfolding, but tonight he was in full flower, confident, funny, and comfortable on stage. At times, when he caught her eye, she returned his broad smile with her own, nodding encouragement. She listened as he cleared his throat and read his last poem, *Ptomaine*.

Tables full of coffee cups,
Empty, full, half full
Crumbs of scones floating
Through the cream.
Look deep within
With your last sip
Not into your soul
But into your cup,
So clean, so free
Of flecks of remnants
Of old donuts stuck
Like scabs on the sides
Of your drained mug.
Thank me. I washed
Each cup in the room
With precision and care.
Stains bleached away,
Lipstick smears wiped clear,
Come fill the cup, drink up,
Talk a lot, lose sleep
Wake up groggy, come back
For a morning cup. It
Revives you, gets you
Moving back for more,
Free of bad old germs
From other lips
And pastry crumbs,
Three days old,
All gone and washed clean
By me, the king of cups,
Who bids you, free

Your mind of fear,
There's no ptomaine
When you drink here.

As if scripted, audience members started a movement of raising their cups, toasting Frankie before the final wave of applause. He bowed with cartoonish exaggeration, collected his poems, waved and shook some hands as he made his way across the room to Ernie's table.

"Bravo," she called out as he took the chair across the table she had been saving for him. "You were so good, so confident. I'm very proud of you."

"You showed me the way, Ernie. 'Write about what you know', that's what you said, and one thing I know a lot about is life in the dish room."

She raised her coffee cup to him. "Life is where you find it."

Before the conversation could proceed, well-wishers began to gather around the man of the hour to congratulate him. He tried to introduce some of the regulars to his cousin but the waitress, Iris, was hovering over her, seemingly desperate to warm up Ernie's coffee.

"No thanks, really, I'm fine," Ernie told Iris over the din of Frankie's new found fans. "I've got to get going anyway."

This caught Frankie's attention. "What? You're leaving?"

"Yes, I've got some things to do back at the house and I've witnessed your triumph." She started to gather up her purse.

Wait," Frankie said, "I'll walk you to your car."

"No need; I'm fine, and you're here with all your friends."

He watched her pull the strap of her purse over her shoulder as she stood up. "No, no, I insist. I really appreciate your being here so it's the least I can do."

Before she could raise further objections, he was on his feet, tearing himself away from the small crowd surrounding him, assuring them he'd be right back.

Once out the door and on the street, Ernie pointed to her car parked at the end of the block and he fell in step with her brisk pace. She unlocked the door and he grabbed the handle to open it for her.

"Thanks, Frankie, you're such a gentleman."

"Aren't I though?" He said, grinning.

"Well, it was a great night for you and I'm glad I was here to see it."

"I'm glad you were too."

As he stood there grinning, she realized he expected a hug. She placed her arm around his shoulder, feeling awkward. He responded with two arms around her waist and held her there for what seemed to her an uncomfortably long time. In attempting to gently release herself, she turned to face him and was met with a kiss on the lips.

She pushed against his chest. "Don't," she said, "Don't do that!"

"I'm sorry. I didn't mean..."

She shook her head. "No, no, no need to apologize. It's no big deal." Her face was stern and empty of warmth as she moved away from him and slid into the car. "Go have fun with your friends. I'll see you at home."

He stared as she drove away and did return to the coffee shop, but only to pick up his sheaf of poems. He mumbled goodbyes to a few of his friends and walked back outside. He kept walking with a heaving chest and a stomach that felt like it was turning upside down. He paid little attention to where he was going. He must have walked a few miles before it occurred to him that he could have stayed with one of his friends from the coffee shop for the night. He could not face Ernie after his stupid, stupid come-on. But it was too late to turn back so he walked a few more miles. He kept checking the time. Ernie was often on her way to bed by eleven. It was pretty close to eleven now. By the time he reversed his course and made it to Effie's house, he was pretty certain that Ernie would be in bed and that he could sneak quietly upstairs to the attic. Had he ruined everything with her, this friendship they had formed, this sharing of common interests, all because he had overstepped his boundaries? What had he been thinking? She was ten years his senior and, if not a blood relative, the amount of family they shared might have made his romantic overture feel like incest to her. A new burning in his face made him feel hot with shame despite the slight chill of the night. He decided he would keep walking till midnight. He was sure she'd be in bed by then.

He was wrong. Despite the dim light in the living room, she was sitting beside a table lamp, reading a book. He blushed at the sight of her.

She moved forward in her chair and closed her book. "There you are. You must have been having a good time with your friends."

He stepped quickly toward her and stopped halfway into the room. "Ernie, I'm so sorry. I'm so ashamed of myself..."

She raised a hand and said, "Stop, please, Frankie. No need to apologize. I'm not mad or offended. I think you're a very sweet boy. It's just that..."

"It's just that I'm still a boy and you're an adult. I know. I should have known. I should have never even entertained the idea. I feel so stupid."

Now she had set her book on the table and was waving her hands back and forth. "No, No, it's not that, although there is something to that, but mostly it's because I think of you as family now and as my very close friend, a thing that's very rare and precious to me. Is it okay for us just to be friends?"

"Okay? Is it okay? It's great. I was afraid you'd ask me to move out."

"Then I would be losing my best friend."

Now she stood up and crossed over to where he was standing. "You know what, Frankie? Friends can hug."

They both reached out and embraced. Frankie had never felt closer to anyone in his life and, in some ways, neither had Ernie.

Ernie was out running errands the next day by the time Frankie came down from the attic. As he walked through the hall past her bedroom, he noticed a book left on her freshly made bed. Though he had no prior intention to enter Ernie's bedroom, something drew him to the book and he walked in. He found a leather bound journal laying there. He started to put it back on the bed, responding to a tug of conscience that proved weak compared to the more powerful tug of curiosity. He opened the book to a random page containing a poem written in neat, legible print entitled

Susan
Your touch caresses my neck
still, after all this time apart.
The trace of soft fingers
felt brushing my cheek.
And when you said, "lie down,
here beside me", the pull
of gravity warring with guilt
and fear and lies of
"I'm not like you,"
even as you drew me down
with kisses from lips
that blew away shame
and satisfied those needs
so long held hostage...

"What are you doing in here?" The combined question and accusation made him slam the notebook shut in mid-sentence and drop it on the bed. He jerked his head toward the door where Ernie was standing and glaring. Before he could apologize or explain what had no good explanation, he blurted out the full shock of his discovery. "You're queer!"

She stepped aggressively into the room. "I'm queer? Is that all you can say? I'm queer. You walk into my room, open up something you have no right to see and then you pass judgment and reduce me to a single word that in your small world tells you everything you need to know about me—'queer'"

"I didn't mean…," he began to stammer.

"You didn't mean to invade my privacy and read things I told you I didn't want to share."

"I…I…, I'm sorry, I…"

"Oh, stop it! I'm sorry? Who are you kidding? You're sorry that you walked into my bedroom or that you read my journal or that you learned something about me that you find disgusting? What exactly are you sorry about?"

"For all of it, for all of it, I'm sorry."

"I'm sorry too. I'm sorry that I'm not attracted to men. I'm sorry that I am attracted to women. I'm sorry that I hate myself for being attracted to women and that, as much as I might want to, I've never felt free to act on it. All I do is write poems and hide them away and hide myself away and stay by myself. I'm sorry. I'm sorry. I'm sorry, and I'm sick to death of being sorry." She turned back to the doorway, put her head in the palms of her hands and sobbed.

Frankie moved toward her but stopped, his whole body clenched like a fist in response to her anger and his stomach churning by what he'd learned from the poem, He had no experience with anything like this except for bad jokes told on playgrounds or locker rooms. He had just entered into an unknown realm.

"Ernie, I…"

She interrupted him with a dismissive wave of her tear stained hand. "No, don't say anything. I can't be around you right now. You're a person I trusted, my best friend. You've ruined that. That's all done now."

When she started running down the stairs he started after her but she turned mid-way and shot him such an angry look that he froze in place. "Not now, Frankie," she said, "not now!"

He watched as she descended the stairs, grabbed her coat from the coat tree in the foyer and left, slamming the door behind her.

He remained in that frozen state, barely breathing, sweat forming on his face and under his arms, heart racing. He forced himself to inhale and felt slightly dizzy. He grabbed hold of the rail at the top of the stairs. The first clear thought that came to his mind was, "I've got to get out of here." He turned and ran down the hall to the attic stairs, racing to get to his duffel bag to begin packing.

The duffel bag was hanging on a hook in a

corner of the attic ready to be quickly stuffed full of clothes scattered on chairs and on the floor. He fumbled for it hurriedly, anxious to be on his way, but it caught on the hook. It was when he turned back to free it that he saw the short hallway dimly illuminated by light from the crack of a door he had never before noticed. As much as he wanted to clear out of the house, his curiosity overcame the flight response. Had he just missed this and never noticed a corner hallway leading to what, another room? How could this be? He knew people at the coffee shop who claimed to have hallucinated after smoking marijuana but he had never tried the stuff. So why was he seeing things? Was he going crazy? All these questions crossed his mind in a confused blur and took his focus away from packing his bag and leaving. He felt drawn magnetically forward toward the door upon which he lightly knocked.

Behind the door, two voices simultaneously called out, "Come in."

He turned the handle and opened the door, peering in before entering.

"Come on. We've been waiting for you," said the heavier man with the shaggy black hair and salt and pepper beard.

"Come in and sit down. How about a nice cup of tea, the other man asked. He was more conventional looking with wavy hair and no beard.

"I'll have a cup, Peter," the first man said.

Peter looked at Frankie and waved for him to fully enter the room. "Allen wants tea," he said, "and

I'm having tea. Surely you'll join us."

Frankie nodded, still reeling from the fight with Ernie, the appearance of the room, and now the presence of these two strange men, one of whom looked strangely familiar. "Sure," he said, slowly approaching the offered chair across from the love seat the two men had been sharing. "Tea would be fine, I guess."

"Oh, no," Allen said, "you can't guess about tea. You can guess about coffee which asks you to consider how wide awake and talkative you want to be. You can guess about alcohol to determine how ridiculously silly you want to act. Tea, on the other hand, enters and leaves the body and the behavior much as it found them. Watch a man drink a cup of tea and you will find no evidence that he has done so."

"Unless he urinates in his pants," Peter said as he approached Frankie with a cup and a tea pot that seemed to suddenly materialize.

"Ah, yes," Allen agreed, peeing is the ultimate equalizer of all human kind. Tea makes you pee."

"And a rose is a rose," Peter added at which the two men chuckled. Frankie smiled politely, not sure what was funny.

"Perhaps, Allen," Peter said, "you should incorporate 'tea makes you pee' into your next poem."

At this, the cloud of confusion blew away and Frankie stared wide-eyed at the bearded man and said, "My God, you're Allen Ginsberg!"

The bearded man, whom Frankie could not help but think of as a roly-poly comic despite the gravitas of his poetry, said, "And exactly what is an Allen Ginsberg, Peter?"

I'm not sure, which is odd since I sleep with an Allen Ginsberg."

"You do?" asked Allen Ginsberg who then turned to Frankie. "And suppose I am this Allen Ginsberg fellow, what would that mean to you?"

Frankie, still trying to process that these two men slept together, simply stared in lieu of a response.

Peter said, "He has no tongue."

Allen said, "I doubt his cousin Ernie would agree with that, Peter?"

Frankie said, "You know Ernie?"

Peter said, "Ah, he has a tongue."

"I have a tongue, yes, but this can't be happening. I've never noticed this room before. It just kind of appeared and, inside, I find Allen Ginsberg and, and…"

"Peter, Peter Orlavsky," Allen informed him. "Peter is also a poet, a very good poet and, I'm happy to say, my lover."

"Your lover?" Frankie took a breath. "Then you're…"

"Queers. We're queers," Peter told him.

"I, I didn't mean, that it…"

"Do queers often make you stammer, young friend?"

"I've never actually met…, not that I haven't

suspected, or I didn't mean to say 'suspected', be-cause, after all, what do I know and, anyway, who am I to judge? Not that anything needs to be judged."

Allen looked at Peter who looked back at Allen and both laughed out loud for several seconds.

Frankie looked from one to the other and then threw up his hands in frustration and a touch of resentment. "Okay, so I'm a dumbbell who doesn't have any idea of what's the right thing to say."

"No, no, you're not dumb." Peter assured him

Allen added, "You don't know what to say be-cause you're a typical young man of our times."

"What do you mean? Is that bad?"

"No, not bad," Peter said, "It's not good or bad, but what is hard is being not typical along with being ahead of your times, like your cousin, Ernie." Now Peter giggled as he nuzzled against Allen. "Don't you just love that name of hers, 'Ernie'?"

Allen squeezed Peter's shoulder. "She's such a delight by any name."

Frankie tried to appear casual in the midst of these displays of male intimacy. "I'm amazed you know Ernie."

"Yes, we know Ernie," Allen said. "She's been up here a lot, especially before you moved in."

"Why didn't she tell me?" Frankie's voice was edged with anger.

"It wouldn't have done any good. People have to discover things that seem unbelievable for them-selves," Peter answered. "And, by the way, why do you think you only just now found this room off the attic you've been living in for several months?"

"I don't know."

"Is it possible," Allen asked, "that it has something to do with the fact that you just now discovered that your cousin is a lesbian?"

"I suppose so, yes, maybe. I don't know. I don't understand any of this. You say I'm a man of my times and that she's ahead of her times. I don't understand."

"Well," Peter said, "a young man in this year of our Lord, 1961, especially one with some tendency toward free-thinking, and a would-be poet to boot, might try to be open-minded about those whom you refer to as queers, but when he runs into the real thing, he's disgusted."

"No," Frankie said, "I'm not exactly disgusted."

"And yet," Peter added, "her love poems will be read someday by a society that, over the years, will come to accept people like us as commonplace."

Allen leaned forward and locked eyes with Frankie. "The accent here is on people—just people, young people, poor and rich people, brave people, frightened people, good people, bad people, and queer people. Homosexuals are people with preferences, just like heterosexuals. And poetry is for people who live and die without noticing the color of a leaf or the pain in the eye of a stranger, except for every now and then when the veil lifts and eternity is glimpsed in a passing cloud."

Frankie was mesmerized by the resonance of Allen's voice. "So a poet's job is to lift veils?"

"Maybe, or to preserve a love of language or to have compassion or to understand each and every person's vulnerability. A poet writes love poems, even if their subject is filth in an alley."

Frankie considered this for a few silent seconds and said, "Ernie writes love poems. She really is a poet. I've just been kidding myself."

"You see, Frankie" Allen said, "that's the problem. Your cousin hides her poetry, hides her heart, hides herself away for fear of her secret being discovered by open-minded, free-thinkers like you who don't judge until it's right in front of their eyes. And when all this is explained to you, you feel pity for yourself because you think we're telling you you're not a poet. Your poems may be clever, may be fun, may even rhyme for God's sake, but until Ernie's pain or anybody's pain matters as much as your own, your poems won't be great."

"So what should I do?"

Peter tucked his arm under Allen's and said, "Love her, care about her and, dammit, get her out to San Francisco where she can thrive!"

The lights in the room dimmed as the entry door blew open. The two figures on the love seat grew less visible. It was time to go. Frankie made his way to the door, down the short hall, and back to the attic. There was so much more he wanted to ask but, when he turned back, there was no hallway, no door.

The reconciliation between Ernie and Frankie took a few strained, awkward days. His apology was accompanied by his assurance that he would move out if she wanted him gone. She said she'd think about it and let him know. She stayed in her room. He stayed in the attic. They were careful to avoid each other at mealtimes and ate in shifts. They each stayed away from common areas like the living room, isolated from one another under the same roof. Before his bizarre encounter with Allen and Peter, he certainly would have simply left. Now, however, having taken their words to heart, he needed her forgiveness and the chance to influence her to find that receptive west coast city where she could live openly as herself and where she would no longer feel like she needed to hide her poetry.

Late on the second afternoon of their mutually avoiding each other, and just before he was going to leave for work, there was a knock on the attic door. Nervously he opened the door and welcomed her in while anticipating that she was going to usher him out.

But she didn't and he apologized again and she accepted and even acknowledged that some part of her may have hoped that he would find the book on the bed and that he would discover her secret.

"Friends like we've become shouldn't have secrets," she said.

"I didn't support your freedom to be yourself. I name-called you. I wasn't much of a friend. I can do better. I will do better."

They smiled and hugged for long seconds. As they separated he said. "I had no right to read your poems, but, my god, you're a really good poet."

"You met Allen and Peter, didn't you?" she asked as they both glanced toward the corner of the attic where no light or hallway door were presently there to be seen.

"I did."

"And did they tell you to compliment me on my poetry?"

"No, that's just me. They told me to encourage you to head west and find the place where you can thrive and where you can share your poems freely with all the people who need to read them."

"They said that?"

"More or less."

"Well, I don't know," she said. "I'll have to think about it. Maybe I've been afraid for too long."

"There are scary people in the world, haters and fools and maybe I've been one of them for too long."

"So we've both got some things to think about."

"And, meanwhile, I've got some dishes to wash."

All of that occurred in 1961. By the spring of the following year, Effie was again back in town. She was between European trips and on hiatus from her volunteer work with UNICEF. There was no one living at the house upon her return

Frankie walked across campus at a fast clip from the parking lot to his ten o'clock creative writing class. Two days earlier his poetry had been read and discussed by his classmates in the loosely structures course which the professor designed to be free-flowing and fun. Frankie had gotten praise from the other student writers and was encouraged by the professor to pursue writing seriously. "Your poetry is good," he told Frankie. "It's real and it has humor and compassion."

Frankie was still glowing from the supportive words but, even more so, from the letter he'd received the previous day at his parents' home. He found living there convenient as he finished his final undergrad year. His father still lounged his days away with cocktail hour arriving earlier and earlier as time passed. His dad's behavior was clearly becoming more and more irksome to Frankie's mother but Frankie was increasingly able to ignore it now that he was committed to his own forward-moving agenda. He paid room and board to keep his dad from calling him a free-loader which Frankie thought pretty ironic as his dad slept while Frankie and mom shared housekeeping chores. He felt good about being there for his mom while he finished college.

From the day he received the letter from

Ernie, he had read it three or four times and had carried it with him in the back pocket of his jeans. Arriving early to the writing class, he pulled it out and read it again.

Dear Frankie,

Sorry I haven't gotten in touch sooner but it's been madness since I moved out here. I was staying in hotel rooms and trying to navigate the bus and train systems. San Francisco is beautiful and exciting but so big it feels like it could swallow you up. But, on the bright side, I'm in my own apartment now and I love it. It's in a section called Haight-Ashbury which is full of off-beat types or should I say beatnik types. I share the place with a woman named Dee Dee who is also a poet. We met at a fabulous book store named 'City Lights' where I was introduced to the owner. He's a poet named Lawrence Ferlinghetti. We chatted and he told me that a friend of his, Allen Ginsberg, had called him from New York and had mentioned my name. Larry asked to read some of my poems. And now for the big news, Frankie: he's publishing a book of my poems. Some advances have been released to what they call the underground press and the reviews have been really positive. This is all so amazing that my head's spinning. Another big piece of news is that I'm no longer hiding who I am. Many of the people I've met here are either attracted to the same sex or to both genders and most of the heterosexuals don't care who you find attractive. Finally, I find Dee Dee very attractive and the feeling is mutual.

Dreams apparently can come true like the dream we both shared of finding that room in the attic at the old house. Was it a dream or a hallucination? I don't know and I don't care.

When I called Aunt Effie, she told me that you've moved home with your parents until you've graduated college. She told me you still read your poems at the coffee shop and are still washing dishes. I'm guessing you won't be for much longer. Get your bachelor's degree, keep on writing, keep in touch, and make your own dreams come true.

Love,
Ernestine

DEACON AND HIS FRIENDS - 1975

Monti handed the joint to Lon and then resumed his pose, arms folded across his chest, leg crossed over the opposite knee. Deacon continued to sketch him, the sketch pad propped open on his knee as he sat on the straight-back, armless chair.

"Oh, gawd, thanks," said the recently arrived Lon. "I needed this. My statistics exam was absolutely impossible. I'm sure I failed it." He brought the joint, pressed between his index finger and thumb, to his lips and inhaled deeply, his pinky finger extended. He coughed, expelling a cloud of smoke, and flattened the palm of his free hand against his chest. "Oh, my Lord, that's strong! I hope you won't mind if, in a few minutes, I begin to act like a complete idiot."

"What makes you think we need to wait?"

Monti asked with a half smile, half sneer.

"Oh, you're cruel," Lon replied as he handed the joint to Angie.

The pretty blonde in the denim mini-skirt, took the joint, studied it, and said," Why not? I'm not working tonight." She took a drag and offered it to Deacon.

He continued his sketching of Monti.

"Deek," she said, "you want this?"

He looked at Angie as if confused by what she was offering. Then he shook his head and returned to the sketch.

"Serious artiste," Lon said. "He never mixes work with pleasure. He should probably seek counseling."

Deacon smiled but continued sketching.

"Don't distract him," said Monti. "I want him to capture me."

Lon felt a jolt of some sensation he could not identify at the idea of a captured Monti but he shrugged it away.

Monti looked at Angie and smiled. She smiled back. "He's so good looking," she thought to herself. "Conceited but damn, he's good looking."

Deacon said, "Monti, hold the pose. Stop smiling. You two can flirt when I'm finished with this."

"Touchy, touchy," Monti said, winking at Angie before reassuming the contemplative expression of the deep thinker. "Are you almost done?"

Deacon ignored the question, made a few

more marks on the sketch pad, a final one with a grand flourish, and announced, "Another masterpiece." He handed it to Monti.

Monti studied it, lower lip extended as he nodded, "Not bad."

Deacon laughed. "For the price, I'd say it's great."

Monti looked at him sharply, "You're going to charge me?"

"No, just kidding."

"Then," Monti agreed, "It's great."

Lon broke in with, "Let me see." When Monti handed the pad to him, Lon studied the sketch with apparent awe as if it were the holy grail. "Nicely done, Deek, but then how far wrong can you go with such a great looking subject."

Angie rolled her eyes. "Lon," she asked, "can't you find a nice guy who shares your interest in guys."

Lon looked hurt. "I don't know what you're talking about, Angie. I'm just making the obvious observation that Monti is a very handsome guy. I'm not saying anything the least bit sexual."

Monti and Angie remained silent as Lon handed the sketch to Angie for her appraisal. Deacon leaned forward in his chair and fired up the roach Monti had left in the ashtray on the table around which they all sat. "I think the work I did on that masterpiece justifies my celebrating another artistic success."

They all laughed as Deacon sucked on the

roach. He inhaled deeply, held the smoke, blew it out and placed the roach in Lon's outstretched hand. Deacon squinted and asked, "You're not high yet?"

"Not high enough," Lon assured him, choking on another deep inhalation.

Angie stood up. "I'm going to open the blinds and let some sun shine in." They all began singing the chorus of "The Age of Aquarius" followed by pot-induced laughter disproportionate to the actual level of humor. Angie walked to the window overlooking the street a story below. She glanced up and down the block and settled on the large, old house across the street. "Funny," she said.

"What is?" Monti asked.

"Most of the houses on this block have been made into apartments; a lot look pretty rundown. But that house across the street looks well maintained: no chipped paint, nice lawn and garden." She turned to Monti. "Is that apartments too?"

"No," he said, "But I've never seen anybody there but a lawn service that comes once a week. Pretty strange." Monti got up from his chair and joined Angie at the window. Lon followed suit as did Deacon who started drawing some lines in his sketchpad."

"It's a beautiful house," Angie said. "You'd think someone would be living there."

"You would," Monti agreed, "but the only time I ever saw anyone but the lawn service people was when a woman came by in a Lincoln Continental. I saw her go in the front door and, a while later, come down the driveway from the back yard. She was looking over the garden along the side of the house, then she seemed to inspect the front lawn. She might be the owner or a realtor. I don't know. She just hopped in the Lincoln and drove off. I never saw her again, or anybody else.

Angie continued to gaze, as if mesmerized by the house. Deacon continued to sketch it. Lon chuckled and said, "I'll bet it's haunted."

"I'm sure it is," Monti said in a mockingly ominous tone, "and I'm sure we should all wait for the next full moon, sneak into the house, have the bejesus scared out of us, and then be slashed to death by a tenant who's been dead for fifty years and only hangs around waiting for the next group of meddlesome young people to kill."

Everyone laughed except Deacon who, after the other three had moved away from the window, continued to sketch the house. Monti said, "I thought you never sketched when you're stoned."

"I usually don't. You have to take some things seriously, but there's something about this house." He remained sketching as Angie put on a Stones album and started swaying to the pulsing rhythm of "Gimme Shelter". Lon joined in the dance as Monti rolled another joint. By the end of the song, Deacon finished sketching with his ritual flourish on the final stroke.

Angie walked back to the window and Lon followed. Both glanced at the drawing and were about to offer their compliments when Angie pointed to a section of the sketch and asked, "What's that?"

Deacon looked at where she was pointing and said, "Probably some sort of attic bedroom."

Angie looked out the window again and then asked to see the sketch. "It's not there," she said.

"What's not there?" Deacon asked.

"This part of the sketch, this room, why did you add it?"

"I didn't add anything that wasn't there."

"No, wait," Lon said, "She's right. Look, Deek."

Deacon looked again at the sketch, especially at the attic bedroom, and then he looked back at the house. There was no attic bedroom. "What the hell," he said. "I'm sure I saw it." His eyes moved from the house to the sketch then back again.

"I'm sure you saw it too," Lon said. "Pot this good, you're bound to see a lot of things."

Monti sat back in his chair and closed his eyes to concentrate on the Stones. Angie and Lon danced in a goofy, exaggerated fashion, laughing. Deacon stayed at the window, staring hard at the house, looking for what he sketched, something that was no longer there.

Deacon was known to smoke a little pot but not often and not very much at a time. His grades were good. He would earn his fine arts degree at the end of the school year. He was a reliable part time worker at a local book store. All of this reassured him that he was not crazy or hallucinatory. So when he looked back at the house and saw the attic bedroom that was not there at last glance, he dropped the sketch pad to the floor and ran across the room, down the stairs, and out the front door of Monti's apartment building.

"Where's he going like his pants are on fire?" Lon asked as he and Angie stopped dancing.

"I don't know," she said. A moment later she walked to the window and saw Deacon standing on the front lawn of the house across the street, looking up. Then she saw him run to the side of the house, still looking up. She watched as he ran back toward Monti's building. In another few minutes he walked back into Monti's apartment. "I've got to get into that house," he said, panting, out of breath.

Monti leapt from his chair. "You mean break in? Why?" This was said with more curiosity that censure.

Angie looked horrified and said, "That's crazy!"

Lon patted Deacon on the back and gave him a sad, patronizing look. "This is the way it always begins, young man: a simple break-in, then armed robbery, then murder, then the electric chair. Mend your wicked ways, my friend, while there's still time."

"It's not funny," Angie snapped.

Lon smiled. "Of course it's funny. Or do you see our resident artist as a cat burglar? Can you imagine our sensitive sketch artist actually breaking into a house?"

"I've got to get in there," Deacon replied with a quiet but firm insistence.

"But why?" Monti asked. "What do you want in there?"

"Look," Deacon said. "Look at what I drew here, up on the roof."

"Yeah, I see it," Monti answered, studying the sketch, "but it's like Lon said. That came out of your imagination, maybe from the pot."

"No, maybe not," Angie broke in as she once more approached the window. "Come over here."

Monti and Lon looked over while Deacon hurried to Angie's side. Then they were all at the window, looking at the house across the street and, more particularly, at the room attached to the roof that none of them, except Deacon, had seen before.

Silence descended on the four of them, a dumbstruck, ominous silence emerging from a shared experience of something inexplicable and frightening.

Monti was the first to break the silence. "You're right, Deak, you do have to get into that house and I'm going with you."

"Wait, you two," Angie said, "There's something weird going on here but there's no reason to get spooked, or to jump off the deep end. This could just be some perceptual glitch, some trick of sun and shadows. Rooms don't just grow on houses and then disappear."

As she spoke, they were all looking at her

except for Lon who, looking back out the window, said, "Oh, no? Well, I've got news for you, science girl, the room just disappeared."

And, indeed it had.

"Let's go," Deacon said and started out the door with Monti close behind. Angie shouted. "Wait!" This stopped them in their tracks.

"Monti," she said, "I can see you breaking into a house. It's within the bounds of your loose sense of morality."

"And thank you very much," he said, eyes rolling.

"It's okay," she said, "it's just you. But, Deacon, it's not you. This isn't in your range, and breaking into a house in the middle of the day is just stupid. It's got to be at night."

Lon snapped his head toward Angie. "You mean you're going along with these two?"

"Of course I am. This needs to be explained. Maybe there's someone in there who's creating some kind of photographic images being projected or some other outlandish thing, but whatever it is can be rationally explained and I want an explanation."

"But the house will probably be locked up tight," Lon objected.

"No problem," Monti said. "Leave it to me. But Angie's right. We'll meet back here at two in the morning. I'll find a way in and you guys will be able to walk right through whatever door I unlock."

Deacon, still feeling a sense of urgency to

have this strange phenomenon explained, guardedly agreed. "Okay," he said, "two in the morning." Even Lon agreed. He didn't want to be thought a coward, despite being petrified about the whole thing.

In the time prior to their reassembling for the break-in, Angie made the wisest choice. She curled up on Monti's couch and let the pot usher her into dreamland. Monti and Lon watched a movie on Beta-Max until Lon fell asleep in his chair. Then Monti left to hit a few bars near campus. Deacon returned to his own tiny apartment and began to reproduce his sketch of the house in oil on canvas.

His eyes moved from sketch to painting repeatedly as he worked the colors to capture the flavor of the red and brown brick house with white shudders and red slate shingles on the roof. He drew the green, terraced lawn and the flower garden along the front of the house. He drew in the fancy brick walkway that snaked from the sidewalk to the front door. With each stroke he felt increasingly automated as if his brush were directed by a force outside of himself and that he was there only as a robot following unspoken commands. At one point it occurred to him that he was no longer referencing the pencil sketch but drawing from memory, although he couldn't say for sure if it were his memory or the workings of a higher commander. He continued in this fashion for four hours and, when the work was completed, if not perfected, he again compared it to the sketch he had not looked at for three of those four hours. He had not missed a thing. He had duplicated the house exactly although it felt strangely as if the house were controlling what he drew.

He always experienced a strong ability to stay focused on his paintings and sketches as he drew or painted. Though his mind could wander at other times his concentration while working was intense. It was different with this painting and, as he cleaned his brushes and put his supplies in order, he reflected on the images that had passed through his consciousness while he was painting and the strong range of emotions that accompanied them.

He saw a young woman running out the front door. He could sense the mixed feelings of captivity and liberation she was experiencing as she walked away. He saw two men cowering as they felt the terror of violent death approaching. Then there were young lovers laughing, talking, and toasting with wine glasses raised high and Deacon felt a warm sensation of strong love that accompanied the vision. Then he saw words on pages floating through the air: pages of poetry, love poetry, humorous poetry. He felt the pain of conflict relieved as it melted into a harmony of support and compassion.

All these feelings and images passed through him as he painted, one fading into another until the last brush stroke. He was all the more convinced that there was a power, some force, inherent in the bricks and mortar, the floors and walls and roof of this house that he needed to discover. With three hours to go before the meet-up with the others he lay back on a recliner and tried to sleep. No sleep came and he merely stared at the painting as those hours passed and it was time to go.

Monti and Lon were passing a hash pipe back and forth when Deacon arrived. Angie was at the window looking out at the house. "You guys are going to get goofy on that stuff when we all need our wits."

"Well," Lon said, "if we each behave like half-wits, you'll still wind up with a whole wit between us."

Monti laughed. "We're going into a house that adds and subtracts rooms while you wait. What better time to get buzzed up?"

Deacon crossed the room to the window and stood next to Angie. "Anybody come or go over there?"

"No, nobody, and the lights are off at both neighboring houses. The whole neighborhood looks like it's asleep."

"That's good." He turned to face the other two. "Okay then, let's go."

They left the apartment and walked quietly down a flight of stairs to the first floor in single file and then onto the front porch. Angie put a finger to her lips just as Lon was starting to speak. "Keep quiet," she whispered. They stole down the front yard and crossed the street. Without having a clear plan, they all followed Deacon to the back of the house. The back yard was nicely mowed with flower gardens planted here and there. All this was visible under the full moon of a clear night. There was a back porch with a row of three basement windows to the right of it and two more to the left. They tried each to discover they were all locked.

Monti said, "Never fear." Then he leveled a patronizing glance at Angie and said, "Maybe I'm high on hash, but I planned ahead." He pulled a small glass cutter from his pocket.

The others stood over him keeping watchful eyes as he bent down and etched a circle into the window glass with the cutter. "Now with a slight tap," Monti said, his fingers upon the glass. The entire pane shattered and fell in on itself.

Angie said, "Way to go, Monti. Why not smoke some more hash?" They waited awhile before anyone made a move. There was silence, with no stirring from neighbors, and complete stillness. Monti reached his hand through the hollow window frame and undid the lock. He looked up as he lifted the window. "Did anybody think to bring a flashlight?"

"I did," answered Deacon. Why don't you get up and I'll crawl in? Then I'll make my way upstairs and unlock that back door to let you guys in. Just be very quiet." He backed in through the window, after clearing away the rest of the shattered glass, and stayed half in and half out till he felt his feet touch the floor. Then he pulled the window shut, turned on the flashlight, and scanned what appeared to be a laundry room. He walked carefully through a doorway that led him into a nicely furnished room with a small bar area, a huge couch and some over-stuffed chairs. At the far end of the room he saw the staircase and followed it up. The door at the top of the stairs was closed and he had a panic moment at the thought that it might be locked. He didn't want to cause any more damage than they had already caused with the window. He breathed a sigh of relief when he turned the handle and the door opened onto the kitchen. He was very near the back door where the others were waiting for him outside. He undid the lock on the doorknob and turned it. The back door opened with a slight creek that seemed excessively loud against the silence they were working so hard to maintain. As the other three entered, Angie was the first to speak. "This is seriously stupid what we're doing here. What if we get caught? We just broke and entered."

"It's fine if you want to leave," Deacon assured her as well as the other two, "but either we were all hallucinating this afternoon or else a structure on the roof of this house appeared and then disappeared and then appeared again. I understand the risk but I've got to find out what's going on here."

"Hey," Monti said in his most nonchalant manner, "my dad's rich because he's a very good lawyer. He won't let his precious son, or his son's friends, do jail time, especially when he convinces a judge it was just a college prank."

"Good," Lon said. "I've never felt happier to be in the presence of a pampered over-indulged child."

"Yeah," Monti agreed, "it comes in handy."

"Okay," Angie said, "let's look and then scat."

Their vision was limited to the range of the flashlight but it was enough to see the large kitchen sink and the appliances: gas oven, large Frigidaire, dishwasher which appeared to be the most modern of the conveniences, waffle iron, toaster, and assorted other gadgets all in their appointed places, all neat and well maintained.

"Should we check out the fridge?" Lon asked, moving toward it.

"We should not check out the fridge," Deacon answered impatiently. "We should stay focused."

"Hey, look," Monti said, "over on the counter." It was another flashlight. He picked it up and turned it on. "Battery's good. Okay, follow me." He led them through a large arched doorway that found them in a dining room with a large hutch full of antique plates, cups, glasses, wine-glasses, bowls, all matched with intricate patterns.

Angie whispered, "Lovely," as her eyes roamed to the octagonal dining table. She crossed over to it and traced her fingers along the surface. "Mahogany is so beautiful."

Then they entered the large room with white sheets covering the furniture and tall, red candles on each end of the long mantle. On the wall above it was a picture of a smiling couple, he very handsome and she very beautiful, pressed close together and dressed in the style of the 1930's. "They look like the people in "The Thin Man" movies. What were their names? Nick and Nora Charles, right?"

"Right," Deacon said, "and their dog, Asta. They drank a lot of gin and solved crimes."

Angie asked, "Did they ever arrest anybody for breaking and entering?"

"Not that I recall," Deacon answered

"Anyway," she added, "it's a lovely room."

"But we need to get upstairs," he told her, "to see about the disappearing room."

"I don't know," said Monti. "I think there's more to explore down here. There's some valuable stuff here I'll bet."

"But it's not your stuff, Monti," Angie said, "and we don't need to add burglary to our breaking and entering rap sheets."

"Perish the thought," he answered with a smirk, but he kept on surveying wall hangings and table ornaments.

Lon said, "I'll keep an eye on him."

"Well, anyway," Deacon said, "you stay down here if you want. I'm heading upstairs."

"I'll go with you," Angie said. "I need to find a bathroom." She followed Deacon to the foyer by the front entrance and then up a flight of stairs. They moved silently over the thick, lush carpeting until they came to the top of the landing. Deacon pointed the flashlight down the hall. Along the way were open bedroom doors and, at the far end, a bathroom. Angie said, "Give me the flashlight and wait for me." He walked her to the end of the hall and did as she requested. She entered the bathroom and closed the door. She rested the light on the sink aiming it at the toilet which she used quickly and then returned to the sink to wash her hands. She didn't want to look at the mirror because she knew the reflection would be shadowy and spooky with the only illumination in the room coming from the flashlight. Vanity overcame fear, however, and she looked at the mirror to check her hair.

She let out a gasp as she saw the strange image reflected in the glass. It was a young woman, clearly frightened, eye make-up streaking down her face, her eyes darting wildly back and forth as if she were anticipating an attack. She was dressed in a loose fitting, flapper dress with beaded embroidery and a long pearl necklace around her neck that swung in time with the startle reflexes that made her body jerk involuntarily. Then the image faded. Angie shook her head as if trying to toss away the fear and panic the image elicited. She hurried out the door, flashlight in hand. When she entered the hallway, Deacon was nowhere in sight but, to her left, there was a door leading onto a flight of stairs. "This must go to the attic," she whispered to herself, as if the sound of a voice, even her own, might reduce her fear. "Deacon must be up there. What was he thinking, leaving me down here alone?" She started up the steps and called out in a low voice, "Deek, are you up there?" She stopped to wait for an answer. When she heard nothing, she was about to head back down until she saw a light at the top of the stairs.

Fear seemed to evaporate as she felt herself inexorably drawn to the light. She reached the top of the stairway. Most of the attic was hidden in darkness except for the strip of light. It came from the crack at the bottom of a door at the end of the short hallway. She moved slowly, not wanting to trip over anything that might be in her path. She walked into the short hallway to the door and tried the handle. The door opened. Angie entered a room full of ornate chairs and couches, a serving tray of various kinds of liquor centrally located, and long, flowing, maroon colored drapes covering the windows. She did not see the woman enter. The woman just seemed to materialize and said, "Come in."

Angie was startled by but not frightened of this woman. "I'm sorry for barging in this way, I just…"

The woman smiled. "Don't apologize. You're welcome here. This is the right place for you to be. My name is Babs."

"I'm Angie."

"Yes, I know. Won't you sit down, Angie?"

Angie took a seat on the couch next to Babs. The latter's clothes were of another era. She looked like a flapper from the Roaring Twenties, a period so often captured in movies. Babs, it seemed to Angie, could have been called up from Central Casting.

"I know I shouldn't be here," Angie said,

blushing at the thought of their break-in.

"No, you should be here. This is your time, Angie. The surprising thing is that I'm here. My time has come and gone, yet, here I am."

"What do you mean, your time has come and gone? It looks to me that we're about the same age."

"Angie," Babs told her, "I was born in 1905."

Now Angie smiled. Please, 1905? You'd be seventy years old."

"I would be. That's correct, but the only time in my life that's important for you to know about is when I was close to your age. That's when something happened that changed my life. I think you already know about it. You saw me in the bathroom mirror a few moments ago, didn't you"?

Angie's eyes widened as she linked this beautiful young woman with the crying, smeared face of the distressed woman she had seen in the mirror in the bathroom downstairs.

"Think back to where you saw me in that mirror, Angie. Close your eyes and think back."

Angie complied, took a breath, closed her eyes, recalled the face in the mirror, and then the rest of it. She heard the abrasive voice of the barrel-chested man calling out for Babs in an insistent, angry voice. She felt Bab's fear. Angie could feel her own heart rate increase as she mentally and emotionally entered into the scene of intended violence and rape. The image came quickly and left just as quickly. She opened her eyes and stared at Babs. "He attacked you?"

"He would have," Babs assured her, "if I hadn't found this room." He was a mobster, involved in all kinds of illegal activity. Years later he was found murdered in this very house."

"By whom?"

"By other thugs and hoodlums, but all that is irrelevant to you. The important thing is that I broke free not only of this house that night but I also broke free of floundering, going this way and that, having to be where the 'fun people' are. Basically I broke free of living like an idiot with no purpose. Earl, that was his name, made me feel vulnerable. I promised myself it would never happen again."

"What did you do?" Angie asked, totally compelled by the story and ignoring or forgetting, for a while, the strangeness of the world in which she found herself.

"I went to college and then to law school, the only woman in my class. I put up with a lot of patronizing and condescending from the male students."

"That must have been awful."

"It was nothing compared to Earl. Anyway, I never felt vulnerable because I chose to surpass them all and I did. I graduated with honors, top in my class. I became a lawyer and when I ran up against exclusively male law firms who wouldn't even interview me based solely on my gender, I opened up my own practice. I wound up taking some of those law firms to court and winning. That's when the offers to join those same firms started coming my way, but I turned them all down and I thrived. Along the way I took on a lot of vulnerable, beaten down, defeated women as clients and helped them find their power."

Angie stared at Babs and said, "What an amazing story." Then she again appraised Babs' 1920 dress and said, "But how can you appear so young at seventy?"

"You're meeting me in my young adulthood. You're hearing this story because you're meant to. Let me ask you something, Angie. How many girlfriends do you have?"

"Girlfriends?" Angie was confused by the seeming non-sequitur. "I don't know. Not many. I find it more interesting to hang out with guys."

"Exactly. Of course you do. Guys are free to behave in ways that are considered socially unacceptable for women. Guys rule the world. They make the rules for themselves and for women. They decide what work is appropriate for men and what is appropriate for women. They go out and experience work and long lunches and private, all male meetings. Men are in charge so why not join them? Why not try to join the club by sharing their opinion that women are second class citizens, full of frivolous concerns, emotionally unstable and in need of male protection. Women who prefer to be friends exclusively with men devalue their own gender."

"I never thought of it that way but, when I listen to you, I have to say, guilty as charged."

Babs smiled and took hold of Angie's hand. "It's not a matter of guilt but of discovery. You came into this house with three young men. You find the self-absorbed one attractive."

"Monti? You mean Monti?" Angie blushed. "I suppose I do."

"But," Babs said, "you immediately knew that the self-absorbed one is Monti."

"Yeah, it's true. He's pretty vain."

"And Lon obviously is not sexually interested in you or any female if he ever gets honest with himself. And Deacon regards you as out of his league, but where's the common thread here?"

Angie shook her head. "I don't know what you mean."

"I mean that you're not their friend, their buddy, just one of the guys. Isn't there something about you being so attractive that gives you admission to the boys club? If you had warts all over your face and weighed three hundred pounds, would you be allowed in the club?"

Angie looked down at the lush oriental rug at her feet without really seeing it, her thoughts going deeply inside herself. "I guess not," she admitted.

"Ever thought about starting your own club and including that homely, overweight girl who just might need someone like you to acknowledge her presence and help her to find her own beauty?"

Before Angie could admit that she had not, the lights dimmed till the room was dark and Babs was no longer present. She sat there amazed at all that was happening until amazement turned to fear and uncertainty as the darkness closed in on her. She turned on the flashlight, got up and made her way to the door and back to the main part of the attic. She opened the door and started down the stairs.

She saw Deacon standing near the bathroom as if he had never left his post.

"Where have you been?" he asked as she exited the stairway.

"Where have you been?" She countered. "I thought you were going to wait for me until I was through in the bathroom."

"I did. I never left."

She was about to object when they heard the sound of stumbling from the end of the hall. They aimed the flashlight toward the sound and saw Lon groping his way through the dark. "Where's Monti?" he asked. "I was right next to him, then he must have walked ahead or lagged behind but, at any rate, I lost him."

Temporarily forgetting the contradictory perceptions of whether or not Deacon had waited for Angie, the three of them began a cursory inspection of the bedrooms. When Monti was not found in any of them, Angie walked back to the attic stairway. Deacon, who had been anxious to get up to the attic to see if he could find anything that would explain the appearance and disappearance of the extra room, took the stairs two at a time. When he got to the top, he was plunged in darkness until Angie and

Lon arrived with the flashlight. None of them saw the hallway in the corner that had led Angie into the room, an experience she was still trying to process before sharing it with the others. She had no idea, nor did the other two, that Monti had found the room that seemed to pull him magnetically away from Lon and had allowed him to float past Angie and Deacon without being noticed. He had climbed the attic steps, seen the light from the hallway which he followed and then opened the door. He was now standing in the room.

He felt like a time-traveler who had found himself transported to a former period of over-stuffed couches and chairs, deal tables. Oriental rugs, tiffany lamps, long, flowing, velvet curtains, and oil painted landscapes hung on dark, green walls. Only one of the lamps was on and the remaining light in the overall darkened room came beaming from the bulb in an antique reel-to-reel movie projector and the image of an old movie it flashed on a bare wall. Monti could make out that it was not a silent film but the sound was muted, barely audible. No one was watching the movie since no one but Monti was in the room. He glanced around until his eyes lighted on an object on an end table next to a glass ashtray. He moved to the table and picked up what he discovered to be a cigarette case that, unless his eyes deceived him, was made of solid gold. His brain immediately began a cost-benefit analysis of choosing to simply slide this valuable object into his pocket. He wouldn't sell it or pawn it. He never lacked for money. It just felt like it was something he should own. He reasoned that this was a big, fancy house, clearly the property of wealthy people who rarely or never lived here and who, consequently, would probably never miss a cigarette case in a room off the attic. He slid it into his pocket.

His body jerked with the startling sound of a voice and a man moving out of the darkness. "Are you sure you want to take that?" asked the tuxedo-clad man coming into the light.

"I...I don't know...I don't know what you're talking about," Monti stammered, trying to hide his shame and his fear. "Where did you come from?"

"Where did I come from? Funny you should ask. I belong here. What about you? Why are you here? To steal things?"

"No, no, I'm not a thief. I just..."

"Hey, kid," the man interrupted, "it takes one to know one. Of course you're a thief or you wouldn't have that cigarette case in your pocket. Now, my question is, do you really want to take it?"

"Okay, you're right," Monti said. "I was going to take this." He pulled the case from his pocket. "But it's just this one time. I'm really not a thief."

"You've got a stolen cigarette case you just pulled out of your pocket, but you're not a thief. I'd have to say, kid, that if you're not one, you're well on your way."

"I'm well on my way to what?" Monti asked, reassuming some of his superior attitude.

"To doing whatever pleases you regardless of

the rules. The rules don't apply to you like they do to other people, do they?"

"Sure they do. I'm not a criminal. You don't know me at all."

I know you, kid. I know you very well. We're what they call kindred spirits, you and me. I always recognize my kinfolk. And, by the way, that cigarette case of mine, you're welcome to it."

Monti's expression brightened. "I am?"

"Sure, what's it to me. I don't smoke anymore. It's one of many things I don't do anymore."

"Wow, thanks, man," Monti said as he slid the case back in his pocket.

"Hold on, kid; hold on a minute. Nothing comes without strings. You've got to earn that case."

"Well," Monti said, with all the sarcasm he could muster, "surprise, surprise."

"Hey, it's no big deal. I just want you to watch something."

"Watch what?"

"I want you to watch the end of this movie," the man told him, pointing to the film being projected on the wall. "Go on, have a seat."

Monti was feeling more in control than when the man had first come into sight and he said, "Sure, why not?" as he slid into one of the overstuffed chairs.

"It won't take long. The film's almost over. Let me turn up the sound." The man remained where he was standing and raised his arm. Suddenly the sound came on.

Monti watched as two men sat side by side on theatre seats in what looked like a private viewing room. The men were silent but the footsteps approaching were loud. Then Monti saw two men enter the viewing room. The camera then panned from the newcomers to the two men sitting silently in their seats. It was then that Monti realized that one of these two men was the man standing near him in this dark room. "That's you," he said to the man.

"Are you sure it's not you?" the man asked just as the two newcomers on the screen leveled guns at the two seated men and shot them through their heads. The two men slumped in their seats, blood splattered all around.

"My god," Monti shouted, "that looks so real!"

"Enjoy the cigarette case, kid." Now the man moved, turning to walk back into the darkness, a big, bloody, gaping hole in the back of his head.

Monti screamed. "Oh Jesus! Oh sweet Jesus!" He flew to his feet, pulled the case from his pocket, and threw it where he had found it on the table. He turned, screaming the name of Jesus, and ran from the room.

The other three had no idea that Monti had gone by them unnoticed on his way to the attic. Angie and Deacon were looking for him on the main floor and Lon, flashlight in hand, was checking the bedrooms on the second floor. He returned to the hallway in time to find Monti racing down the attic stairs, running into the flashlight beam and shouting, "Unreal, unreal, can't be real. Oh Jesus, Jesus, Jesus."

Lon reached out to grab him. "What's the matter?"

Monti stopped long enough to display a face pale white from fear. "Up there." He pointed to the attic stairs. "It can't be real." Immediately Monti pulled away from Lon's loose grip, ran passed him, and down the stairs to the main floor. Lon, upended by seeing the cock-sure, supremely cool Monti wailing on insanely, remained standing in the hallway. He started down the stairs but, prompted by curiosity and the sense of security against the darkness afforded by the flashlight in his hand, turned and made his way up the attic stairs. The light from the hallway greeted him and he walked slowly toward the closed door. He touched it gently before knocking but it opened on its own. He walked into the room with sparse furniture including a wingback chair and a side table with a reading lamp. Across from the chair a woman sat at a card table upon which were stacks of paper and another lamp. The woman had a pen in her hand and what appeared to be a leather-bound notebook opened before her.

She looked up and smiled. "Come in, Lon. Have a seat."

He hesitated for a moment wondering what it could have been that reduced Monti to a frightened mess. Surely it couldn't have been this pleasant looking woman. As he sat down it occurred to him that she had called him Lon. "How do you know my name?"

Avoiding a direct answer, she said, "It's so strange for those of us who have discovered this room. It's unlike anything any of us have ever experienced in the worlds we're used to."

"What do you mean? It's just a room, isn't it?"

"Why would you think that, Lon? Aren't all of you here because your friend sketched this house which included an addition on the roof that none of you saw when you first looked at the house? Then you all did see it and then you didn't. Isn't that what brought you here?"

"Optical illusion. Play of light and shadows." He raised his arms and let them drop to his lap. "Oh, I just don't know what it was. Maybe I'm dreaming."

"Maybe you're not."

The vague and confusing responses Lon was getting from her began to frighten him. "I'm feeling a little spooked here." He started to get up from the chair. "I think I should go."

"Alright, Lon, if you choose, but sometimes it's good to talk to someone with similar preferences."

He felt his spinal column jerk. "Preferences? What do you mean?"

"Well, naturally, I mean it's sometimes good to talk to other homosexuals."

Lon's body sprang upright and he sat at attention on the edge of the chair. "What are you talking about? I'm not gay."

"But of course you are, Lon. Don't you say sexually suggestive things to Monti?"

"That's joking. I'm just joking. I act kind of silly and it gets a laugh but I'm certainly not a homosexual."

The woman stood up and moved toward Lon. She placed a hand on his shoulder. "I'm sorry for you because I know how hard it can be to come to terms with this. The truth is that you are gay and in the back of your mind you know it."

He was about to object again but something about her hand on his shoulder was so soothing, so gentle, that he simply started to cry.

"It's okay," she assured him in a soft voice. "It's okay and it's going to be better. I came out fifteen years ago but not until I moved to San Francisco and found a loving, supportive community. It's not necessary to do that now. There's still lots of stigma but it's getting better and it's going to keep getting better as long as we all stop hiding."

"But what'll people say?"

"Some will say awful things, stupid things, mean things. Others will feel awkward around you but they'll try to understand. The ones you need to be with are the ones who need your support so they can support you in turn."

"I don't know if I'm ready."

"You'll know when you are. You'll know because you'll be tired of hiding and feeling shame and feeling inferior. You'll know when you tap into the strength required to accept yourself with pride and stop paying attention to the haters. You'll know when it's time."

He sat there wiping tears from his eyes. She removed her hand from his shoulder.

"Do you like poetry?" she asked.

"I don't know. I guess so. I don't read much of it."

She went to the desk and returned with a book. "This is one of my collection of poems. I've published others but this is my first. They were all hidden away in a journal for years before a friend found them. He helped me realize I was hiding my truth from the people who needed to hear it. Maybe you'll read them, maybe not. I can only say that I'm proud that they're out there and no longer hidden. I'm proud that I'm no longer hiding. That's what I wish for you."

He took the book and held it for a moment. The light next to his chair went out. She walked back to the desk. Then the desk lamp went out just as the opening door called to him. He followed his flashlight back to the attic and slowly descended the stairs.

He found the others in the foyer on the first floor. Deacon was listening to Angie who was describing her meeting with the young woman she had met in the attic room. Monti was breathing heavily, working hard to find some relief from his fear. He waited until Angie had finished to tell of his experience with the murdered man with the hole in his head. Lon listened to the story as he came down the stairs to the foyer. He wrapped an arm around Monti in an attempt to calm the fear. Monti did not resist. He continued his deep breathing until he felt a bit better. "I just have to accept that I was hallucinating. That's all. I was hallucinating but oh sweet Jesus, I've got to repair that window I broke."

The other three looked at him. Could this really be Monti, worrying about repairing damage he caused. Monti had good pot, a nice apartment where they could smoke it, an attractiveness that drew people to him, but he was never one to appear overflowing with conscience.

Angie seemed subtly different as well. She seemed a little distant from the others. The three young men could have no way of knowing that they would be seeing less of her, that she would be switching her major soon to Women's Studies and making new female friends.

On the other hand, Lon's experience in the room was shared in a way that spared the other three any guesswork. "I have to let you all know something about me. I'm gay."

Deacon simply nodded. Angie said, "We know." Monti pulled away from Lon's arm on his shoulder but gave him a friendly pat on the back. "Hey, man," Monti assured him, "you're okay with us. We don't care what you are."

"I think we should get out of here," Angie said. Monti and Lon agreed but Deacon had not yet seen the room. The others said they would wait for him as he turned and walked up the stairs.

Fifteen minutes later found Deacon returning slowly down the stairs. His expression was neutral, surprising to the other three given their emotions after their respective experiences in the room. At the bottom of the stairs he shrugged and said, "There was nothing."

"Nothing in the room?" Angie asked.

"No room," he answered, "not that I could see."

"You think we're all crazy?" Monti's voice was still shaky. It was not a defensive question, just a question.

"Three of my friends tell me they saw something. I believe you all did," Deacon assured them. "As soon as I got to the attic I knew I wouldn't see anything. I just knew. I just stood there for awhile wondering why."

"Maybe you have to believe the room exists to be able to see it," Lon suggested.

"Did any of you?" Deacon asked.

They admitted they hadn't

"I believed from the beginning," Deacon said. "I was the one who first decided to go looking for an explanation. I needed to know why I drew something that wasn't there. I believed something was there at the time and I believe each of your stories."

"Then why couldn't you see it?" Angie asked.

"It doesn't matter," Deacon answered, smiling. "I think I was very lucky. How many people really, truly believe in things they can't see? People pray and preach and thump their holy books but almost every one of them experience that doubt that comes like a panic attack in the middle of the night. But me? I absolutely believe in something I can't see. I sketch, I paint, I duplicate the appearance of things. I'll just keep on drawing what I see and hope someday that I'll break through the surface, or feel like I have. Maybe then I'll walk into a room of my own.

Angie moved close to Deacon and hugged him. Lon approached Monti to hug him but Monti immediately said, "I love you, man, but let's just shake hands."

Lon laughed. All of them laughed until Angie raised a finger to her lips to shush them as she opened the front door. Then the four of them went silent, crossed the threshold, and walked into the pre-dawn with the barest trace of sunlight rising in the distance.

EFFIE - 1993

She was 78 years old now and, though she still owned the old house, she rarely came by. She lived now in a high-rise, mid-town apartment building, on the top floor. She kept a roof garden and had a grand view of the river. She had spent much of her time and money in the service of UNICEF. She had made thirty-seven trips overseas, had seen a lot of suffering first hand, and had done what she could to alleviate it. Now though, she was no longer up to the rigors of travel. Having earned the respect of other volunteers and professional staff, she was still consulted and asked for advice. She was respected for her support from friends she'd made in the military and for encouraging doubled and re-doubled effort to find Jimmy. She hired private investigators and questioned police departments of cities and villages where American soldiers had served. No one could offer any hope.

While continuing her search, she started her

volunteer work, first with CARE, then with UNICEF. She was not about to reduce herself to a feverishly insane woman on a desperate and perhaps futile mission. The charity work offered her a useful purpose. The searching was ongoing but on the side.

A part of her accepted the likelihood that he was dead, but the question continued to nag, "How could a person pulsating and vibrating with so much life have vanished? She knew the simple answer, that he was another casualty of war, but to have embraced the vitality, the spirit, the fun of him for so few years and then to live with his memory for so many more made him loom, in her mind, as larger than war, larger than events and statistics. That force of nature, she was certain, must still exist somewhere.

Yet, she had made her last trip overseas. She had not found him. She was beginning to feel a certain truth that was painful knowledge. As long as she looked, he was, for her, someone who still remained in this world. Now, with her arthritis, some respiratory problems, and a few other inconveniences, she was accepting that her time in this world was winding down.

Thoughts of Jimmy and aging and time ran around in her brain as she pulled her car into the driveway of the house that, until a few years ago, had been her home when she was not travelling. It was the only well cared for house on a badly blighted block. Despite all the care, her house, along with twenty-three other houses in the old neighborhood, had been taken over through eminent domain in order to accommodate a mega-hospital expansion.

She was not terribly saddened by this turn of events. She knew her memories resided in her mind, not in the house. It had had an interesting history, not only for her and Jimmy, but for some relatives. Her nephew, Frankie, had needed a place to stay some years back as had Effie's cousin, Ernestine. They actually shared the house for a time and had become good friends. Frankie was now teaching English Literature at University and Ernestine had distinguished herself as a notable, nationally known poet, living in the Bay Area. Effie was glad she was able to have helped them on their way. She was grateful to have owned the house and happy to have it uprooted to make room for a hospital. This would be her last visit.

She entered through the front door, the threshold over which Jimmy had carried her so many years ago. It felt like only moments ago as she stood in the foyer, recalling. She walked through the living room reminiscing about snuggling on the couch, making plans, drinking wine, laughing. In the kitchen she recalled quick snacks and cheese sandwiches between lovely love-making sessions. Then she returned to the foyer and started up the first flight of stairs. Stairs were not easy for her now with the arthritis and some shortness of breath. She came to the top of the stairway and walked past the first bedroom and then to the master bedroom. She felt tears forming as she looked at the bed and all that it brought to mind.

She felt tired, unbelievably tired. It surprised her. She had not felt tired as she drove to the house but now she felt exhausted. Her breathing continued to be difficult. She felt her heart pounding. No matter, she told herself, because she still had another flight of stairs to master. She continued down the hall and stopped at the door that led to the attic. Would she see the room, the magic room? She had to know.

Her breathing was more strained with each step until, halfway up the flight she stopped, uncertain as to whether she would make it to the top. She was operating now on sheer force of will but she continued to climb until, at the top, she looked ahead and saw the light, the hallway, and the door. She moved forward and entered the room.

"Hi, sweetie." He stood there in the middle of the room. Champagne was in an ice bucket on a table beside him. He looked exactly as he had looked the last time she had seen him.

"Jimmy," she cried out, running into his outstretched arms. She no longer felt short of breath; she only felt the warmth of his embrace, his kiss on her lips. She suddenly felt self-conscious. How could he be kissing such an old lady? The she saw her reflection in the mirror over his shoulder, the image of a young woman, a young Effie. The years had vanished. She began to cry.

"Now, now," he said, "no cause for tears.

Aren't you glad to see me?"

"Oh, I'm so glad, Jimmy. I looked for you for so long, for so many years, on so many trips. I'd given up." She clung to him more tightly.

"None of that matters now, all that's behind us. They kissed and embraced and neither wanted to let go. Then he said, "Let's celebrate. I brought champagne, your favorite kind."

"I see that," she said, "I just don't want to let go of you to drink it."

"I know; I feel the same way, but, Effie, we've got an eternity to be together."

She looked up into his eyes and then she knew. "Yes," she said, "eternity." She released him and he poured the champagne. He handed her the glass and she said, "To us."

He said, "And to our journey."

"Journey?" she asked but needn't have. She knew where they were and where they were going. She knew that workmen who were coming to tear down the house would find the body of an old lady halfway up the stairway to the attic.

They sat on a love seat, snuggled together, and sipped champagne. "Is it nice where we're going?" she asked.

"Oh yes," he told her. "It's wonderful. I've been there for a long time. I've just been waiting for the right time to come back for you. I wanted to come sooner but then you couldn't have accomplished all that you did. You had too much value to add to the world for me to come and snatch you away before it was time."

She held his hand tightly. Outside came the sound of loud engines and metal bouncing against steel and concrete, men's voices, heavy hammer blows, footsteps on the roof, shingles ripped and falling down the sides of the house. "Is it time to start our journey?"

"It is, Effie; it's time to go."

"I'm ready."

The light in the room faded into shadows. The men working inside the house found a body on the attic stairs. An ambulance came. The deconstruction was halted for a day but resumed the day after. The house came down beam by beam, brick by brick, scrap hauled away until, within a few days there was only the empty lot awaiting new construction.

Made in the USA
Las Vegas, NV
10 October 2021